THE INFLUENCERS

KASSANDRA GARRISON

I.

ORIGINS

Darkness consumed me. The kind of inescapable darkness that overwhelms a person's senses. I fight harder and harder to become aware of my surroundings. It was as though I were fighting to break the surface of the water, its forceful current taking me deeper and darker than before. As my eyes flickered open to reveal light, they felt much too heavy to keep open, losing consciousness yet again.

My dreams had become vivid, too surreal. Images of my childhood began running through my mind. My mother, her soft brown hair blowing in the breeze, placing the food on a blanket for our picnic. Sandwiches, apples, and bottles of water litter the cloth. We had a picnic the same day every year: the day of my father's death.

He was a soldier in the military, high honors and countless medals. On a mission overseas, his location was discovered by a terrorist cell and the soldiers were ambushed. Being greatly outnumbered and outgunned, no soldier survived. A hero's funeral was given for him where we had lived in Virginia.

My mother recalls holding me in her arms, an infant at the time, and accepting the flag that lay on my father's casket. The sound of rifles nearby in salute to her fallen soldier.

With a newly born baby in her arms, she had begged my father to stay upon hearing of his impending deployment. Having no other choice, my father kissed my mother and I goodbye for the last time before boarding the plane. She recalled that day on her death bed, eagerly awaiting their reunion that ought to have occurred eighteen years ago.

Suddenly, I was drawn out of my memories as an abrupt burst of acid reached my tongue. I vomit uncontrollably, heaving severely on my side and tasting the bitterness of the bile emptying from my stomach. I hear voices, a man and a woman. All at once, there are hands gently pulling me up from the surface where I lay.

Though they struggled to focus clearly, my eyes gradually lost their oppressive heaviness and allowed me to recognize objects. The rough sheets that scratch the surface of my skin are a stark white made alarmingly brighter by the fluorescent lights overhead.

There are two dark figures leaning over me with their hands firmly grasping my arms as my body trembles. My senses are dulled, making it difficult to focus on the faces of the individuals holding me up. The hands guide me to lay back down on the crisp sheets, brushing my hair away from my sweat-ridden forehead.

Tremors and chills run through my body as my stomach threatens to empty itself again.

She needs fluids right away. Dwayne, please, go get one unit of intravenous fluids from the back.

The sound of feet hitting the hard floor grows quieter, interrupted by the sound of a door closing firmly as the man named Dwayne retrieves the requested fluids. I blink my eyes hard to focus on the face of the woman standing beside me.

In a white lab coat that envelopes her small frame, a middle-aged woman with soft features and red hair smoothed into a bun calmly studies me. Bringing the stethoscope from around her neck, she places the cold metal on my chest and quietly listens to my heartbeat. She then places a blood-pressure cuff around my arm and writes down the results on a pad of paper laying on a nearby table. Dwayne returns with a clear bag of fluid, hanging it on a metal hook.

The woman has already grabbed my hand and begun inserting the needle into my skin for the IV. The pain was sudden and sharp, a quick gasp escaping my lips. Her eyes flicker to my face before she places tape over the needle and connects the bag of fluid to the IV.

That is all, Dwayne. You may leave.

Dwayne nods and retreats across the small room, exiting through a heavy metal door. The woman pulls a stool next to the slim cot where I lay.

3

My name is Evelyn. I am the head nurse of this institute. Can you tell me your name?

My throat is dry and only a raspy squeak escapes my lips. She passes me a small paper cup with tepid water, patiently waiting for me to sip the water and answer her question. I can feel the coolness of the intravenous fluids as they enter my body, traveling up my forearm.

Darcy. Darcy Bishop.

It is a pleasure to meet you, Darcy. I will read a quick summary of your basic personal information. Stop me if there is anything incorrect. You are eighteen years old, natural golden hair, blue eyes, and you are an orphan.

Her last statement feels like a stab to the chest and I wince as the reality of that statement sets in. Seeing my hesitation, she studies my face with slight concern.

Is this correct?

I nodded in agreement and watched her scribble notes on her pad of paper.

Do you have any current illnesses or history of family health conditions?

Well, I don't feel so hot right now, but I have no health problems. If you don't mind, may I ask why you are asking these questions? And, where am I?

The questions begin to flow as I find my voice and realize the oddity of it all. She seems slightly unnerved by my incessant questions but pushes on.

Your questions will soon be answered. However, I am required to verify your personal information before moving onto the next step in the process. Does your family have any history of diseases or mental health problems?

The room that we occupy is small and white with a table close to the small stretcher on which I laid. Other than the stool, the room remains empty. Realizing I have no other choice, I return my gaze back to the nurse beside me.

Breast cancer. My mom had breast cancer.

Evelyn continues her writing on the paper before setting it down on the table beside her. Hands clasped in her lap, she maintains eye contact with me. Her skin seemed almost porcelain, tiny freckles scattered across her nose. Though her features were soft, her dark eyes seemed to pierce beyond superficial vision.

You have been recruited by a secret society called the Influencers. Once we verify that you are healthy, you will be entered into the training program here. For the next 2 hours, you will receive intravenous fluids and later undergo a physical, including a weighing and reflex check.

Training? Training for what?

Depending on your skills and abilities, you will be placed into a specific role chosen by the Board.

Wait. You said I was recruited. I didn't sign up for this.

I—

My words came to a sudden stop as the reality of how I got to this place flooded into my memories. After my mother passed, I had moved into a small apartment afforded only by my mediocre job as an office assistant at a real estate office. I had woken up early enough that spring morning to take a run before work. Walking out my front door, a man drove by in a dark sedan. He glanced my way several times but seemed only to be observing his surroundings.

I locked my apartment door and proceeded to the sidewalk. Placing my iPod on shuffle and the earbuds in my ears, I began jogging at a steady pace toward the park. The streets leading to the park were quiet at that time in the morning. Being a small city, the town of Furlow, Oregon, had a nostalgic atmosphere with classically restored buildings downtown and old-fashioned streetlamps.

Though an avid fan of sleep, there is something beautiful about the morning. The quiet streets, the fresh cool air, and the earth waking up from its slumber. It's as if the world is new and the day has only begun, holding opportunity for new beginnings.

I feel the sweat dampen my temples as I near the park. Though several blocks from my one-bedroom, one-bathroom apartment, I feel a certain connection to this park. The park where every picnic with my mother took place. She would always lay the stereotypical red-checkered blanket in the field overlooking the river.

There was a veteran's memorial built close to the water with columns commemorating each branch of the military. Though she tried to make every picnic a celebration of my dad's life, the columns in the memorial would always catch her eye. Her brown eyes would become distant, as if visualizing the past: a time without an unending and aching emptiness in her heart, a time when she was complete.

Every time she would gaze in the distance, she would return to reality quickly and look down at me, her eyes glossy. Her soft tanned hand would cup my chin with a look in her eyes of bittersweet remembrance.

You look so much like your father. Your eyes and hair come alive in the sunlight, too.

She would then clap her hands and begin picking up the remnants of our lunch. Before heading back to the car, she would take me through the veteran's memorial and stand in front of the pillar holding the military branch to which my father belonged. A flower from the picnic basket would be placed at the foot of the pillar, a single blue hydrangea. Standing solemnly beside the monument, my mother would reminisce on that flower.

My father and mother had been living from apartment to apartment in various cities for years. Finally, my father received news that he would be stationed permanently at the Langley Air

Force Base in Virginia. After weeks of owning their very own home, my mother still felt as though it was merely another temporary residence.

Her hometown in Oregon had been landscaped with beautiful flowers including hyacinths, rose bushes, irises, lilies, and her favorite: blue hydrangeas. Upon returning home one afternoon from the store, my mother found the back door open.

Cautiously, she looked around the house, expecting to find an intruder in her home. She made her way through the kitchen and out the back door toward the fenced yard. In awe, she stood looking at the dozens of blue hydrangeas that my father had planted in their flower beds. Their sweet smell filled the air as she ran to my father with tears escaping her eyes, finally feeling as though they were home. Surrounded by her favorite flower and the arms of the man she loved, my mother realized that he was her home.

Coming back to reality, I realized that I had run far beyond the view of the monument along the water's edge. Too much time had gone by and I needed to get ready for work. At a hurried pace, I made my way back to my apartment. Entering the front door, I threw my iPod and keys on the kitchen counter and hurried to my bedroom.

Suddenly, everything went black. A coarse material had been thrown over my head, strong hands grasped my arms and restrained my attempted kicks. Breath filled my lungs as I gasped for air in panic. I swung my arms in an effort to stun my attacker, my elbow connecting with the soft socket of an eye. A deep voice cursed, and the attacker loosened his grip. Falling to the ground, I reached to take the hood from my head. Suddenly, I felt a prick on my arm and then darkness engulfed me.

It was as if Evelyn knew my very thoughts as she studied my body language and facial expressions. She seemed prepared for a beating as reality weighed like a ton of bricks on my chest.

I wasn't recruited at all. I was kidnapped! You broke into my apartment and took me! I didn't sign up for this and I don't know why anyone would. So far, I've been kidnapped, drugged, and questioned about my personal history, which might I say is none of your business. I'm done with the questions. Let me go.

I am afraid that it is far too late for that, my dear. After being chosen and... recruited..., you have no other option than to enter the training program and be placed where they shall choose.

Like he—

I am sure that you will find the program most rewarding. For now, you will finish replenishing your fluids, spend one more night, and complete the physical before being assigned a room. No other questions will be asked at this time. That is all.

I stared in disbelief as Evelyn checked the level of intravenous fluid calmly and walked out the heavy metal door, letting it slam loudly behind her. I had to get out of here. But I had no idea where I was. If I could pass the physical and be released from this room, I could look for an escape and call the cops.

But who was going to believe me when I claimed that I was abducted by a secret society wanting to train me to be their puppet? Deep in my soul, I just knew that I needed to get out. All I had to do was make a plan.

II.

SMOKE AND MIRRORS

After finishing the fluids and enduring restless sleep through the night, Evelyn returned with a sad excuse for nutrition. Two packets of crackers lay on a tray next to a glass of water. Though I didn't completely trust the nurse, my dry throat and empty stomach forced me to quickly consume the small rations.

Studiously, I inspected the seal on the cracker packaging, eyeing the nurse as I took my first bite. Evelyn waited patiently before guiding me through the physical where she measured height, weight, blood pressure, flexibility, vision, and hearing. She scribbled the results down between each test and remained silent.

She exited the room without a sound and returned after several minutes. Evelyn held in her hands clothes and a syringe with a sizeable needle.

Hold on. You're not sticking that in me, are you?

Do not be afraid. The size of the needle is necessary for the tracking device to be placed safely under the skin.

A tracking device? Am I a dog?

Evelyn did not seem amused at all by my wit. Instead she placed the stack of clothes beside me on the cot and grabbed my left arm. The needle entered my inner arm near the bicep, leaving behind a miniscule lump. Evelyn placed a band aid over the puncture wound and looked into my eyes.

From now on, you will be able to be tracked anywhere that you may go. They will know if you disobey orders or if you try to escape. You belong to the Society now. Welcome, Darcy Bishop, to the rest of your life.

With that, she instructed me to get dressed in the clothes she provided and wait for the placement officer. The clothes were a pair of charcoal gray jogging pants and a white V-neck. Tennis shoes were left beside the bed with a pair of socks. Shortly after I was completely dressed, a tall, burly man in all black entered the room.

Darcy Bishop, my name is Stanley. I will be your placement officer and your guide through the facility today.

His dark brown eyes held a unexpected kindness as he reached out his hand to shake mine. Though confused, I hesitantly reached my hand out and shook his. Seeming pleased with the greeting, Stanley opened the heavy metal door with ease and motioned for me to exit the room.

The hallway was white as well, with the absence of color giving the environment a feeling of sterility and coldness. Stanley walked down the corridor past identical doors until he reached the end of the hallway where an ID scanner was placed on the wall. After scanning his card, the double doors at the end of the corridor slowly opened into a large room.

The room had a modern interior design. Furniture at the far end of the foyer, a black leather material covered every sectional and glass acted as every tabletop. A wet bar was placed on the opposite side of the room with a coffee maker, cups, and sugars organized neatly on the granite countertop. Stanley verified my presence before continuing through the great hall into the next corridor.

This great room was designed to encourage unity within the Society. Many of the nurses from the unit will gather here before and after work to have small talk or relax after their shift is complete. This hall leads to a restricted use elevator which then leads to the executive suites. These offices belong to board members and to the President of the Society.

Stanley once again paused at the end of the hall. Pressing a silver button on the wall, elevator doors opened to a small space made completely of glass. Through the glass, the outside could be seen. As far as the eye could see, desert sand and dried shrubs covered the land.

However, the climate of the region was not the greatest shock by far; it was the distance to the land below us that was most fearsome. Hundreds of feet stood between the elevator and the arid land below. All at once, I realized the distance from home I had been taken.

No longer the impressive forests and lush landscape of my small hometown in Oregon, this desert must have been hundreds of miles away from home. Looking out the window at the lack of civilization or signs of life, it was evident that the facility was in the middle of nowhere.

Stanley seemed to realize my shock at the surrounding landscape. He shifted his feet and cleared his throat before looking down at my frozen face.

It is a much prettier sight at sunset. The colors of the sky seem to bring life to the scorched earth.

Still speechless, I only nodded and returned my gaze to the horizon. A beeping noise filled the elevator before the metal doors opened to a formally decorated hallway. Pieces of artwork filled the neutrally painted walls and small decorative tables held flower arrangements.

Only a handful of doors littered the hallway with one labeled "Conference Room" and others presumably with names of board members. The rooms, with their doors shut, showed no signs of habitation this early in the morning. However, one room at the end of the hall offered a sliver of light between the door and the carpeted floor.

Stanley guided me toward the occupied door, knocking softly on the door.

You may enter.

Stanley opened the door, directing me to enter the room. The curt voice belonged to a woman who stood by the windows of her office, arms clasped behind her back as she faced the desert.

She had dark brown hair that was tightly wound into a bun on the back of her head, not a tendril of hair free from its clasp. She wore a gray pant suit that was absent of any wrinkle or imperfection, delivering the feeling that she was a businesswoman first and foremost.

Turning to greet us, I found her face to be nearly as rigid as her choice of outfit. Underneath her serious demeanor and style, she had a sort of elegant beauty about her. She nodded to Stanley who then retreated out of the room and closed the door behind him.

Her focused eyes fixed on me. Quietly, she stood and scrutinized me from head to toe. Seeming neither pleased nor disappointed, she walked to sit behind the large desk in the middle of the office. The executive style desk was a dark wood, with sharp lines and a lack of frilly decoration. The two were a perfect match.

Darcy Bishop, my name is Margot Clarke. I am the President of this Society. Please have a seat.

She held her hand toward a high-backed leather chair placed in front of her desk. Hesitantly, I walked across the room and sat in the oversized chair. I couldn't help but think she chose such a large chair to make her subordinates feel even smaller.

The Society was created in an attempt to help change the world for the better. By placing advocates from our secret government into all aspects of civilization, we can somewhat control events in the world. Our goal is to create peace and to cure all diseases. *Without the members of our Society, we would not be able to make this positive impact on the world.*

She paused to take a sip from the coffee cup on her desk. Lifting her elbows onto her desk, she clasped her hands together and focused intensely on me.

This is why you are here. For the next four months, you will be trained in various subjects including various languages, etiquette, cultures, and the arts. You will use this knowledge to succeed in the position in which we place you. After we are sure you blend in nicely, you will begin to receive orders from the Board. Do you have any questions, Darcy?

Her gaze was so intense and information so unbelievable, I was at a loss for words in the first moments of silence. She waited patiently for me to speak.

Why does this Society have to be secret if it is trying to help the world?

Darcy, in order for this Society to succeed, it must be free from any established governments. If our group is restricted by the same governments that run the world, then there would be no difference made, only the same decisions they are already making. We strive to be an independent government who merely nudges others in the right direction without any awareness of its planned intentions.

The President had a certain air about her. As she explained the purpose of the Society, her words seemed to allow no room for falsehood. Her body language, the way she sat straight as a board and the confidence in her every move, left no room for doubt. Hazel eyes, appearing to be nearly the same color of her pant suit, were fixated on me as I sat frozen in place.

So that is your excuse for kidnapping young girls from their homes?

If she was caught off guard, there was no sign of it in her flat eyes and arrogant posture. She merely picked up her coffee mug and proceeded to stare at me over the rim without batting an eyelash. Carefully, she lowered the glass and placed it on the desk.

You see, Darcy, it would not be a secret if we posted a help wanted ad in the newspaper. Besides, after a few weeks here, I believe that we can change your entire perspective on the Society. In fact, you may find yourself in awe and loyal support of its benevolent mission.

I doubt it.

All at once, her demeanor changed. Her eyes darkened and she sat forward in her chair. Eyes cutting into the deepest part of my soul, she spoke through pursed lips.

Darcy, I would change my attitude if I were you or your training might prove to be extremely challenging. Stanley will take you now to your flat.

She pressed a button on her phone before the door opened and Stanley walked in. He kept his head low in respect to his superior. Directing me to stand, Margot dismissed our presence, placing her reading glasses on her face and shuffling papers on her desk.

Back in the hallway, Stanley once again began walking toward the elevator doors. As always, he remained stoic and calmly guided me where I needed to go. The elevator shifted as we descended back to the ground level.

So, do you believe all this "secretly helping the world" bullcrap?

A smirk crossed over Stanley's face as the elevator doors opened. He put his hand over the sensors to prevent the doors from closing on us. Stubbornly, I stood still and waited for his answer. He seemed to comprehend that his answer was the key to me exiting the elevator.

Every new recruit...

Victim.

He patiently sidestepped my correction to his statement and calmly proceeded with his answer.

Every new recruit has their doubts and angry feelings when they first come to the Society. However, many of them change their minds in a manner of a few weeks. You will find the Society to be quite hospitable and generous. I will now show you where your flat is located.

His hand remained blocking the elevator door as it began warning its passengers with an annoying buzzer. Seeing the kindness and patience in his eyes, I conceded and exited the elevator. Besides, I was still weak from whatever medicine they knocked me out with and sincerely hoped that they provided me with a bed in this "flat" they spoke of.

However, I couldn't help but notice that Stanley and Evelyn both seemed to have the same calm demeanor as they did their jobs. A chill swept up my back and left chill bumps on my arms as I thought of how very similar everyone acted here... as if brainwashed into believing they were a part of a greater cause. A cause that required submissive followers.

III.

THE DESERT FLAT

My flat belonged to an entire building of identical doors, each with their own assigned number. Mine was at the very top of the building on the fifth floor. As Stanley opened the door labeled 58, I stood in awe of the room before me.

The floors were made of hardwood and the walls painted a creamy white. Eclectic lights hung from the ceiling in the middle of the room over various couches and a large coffee table. The couches had blankets and throw pillows scattered across them while the table held a vase full of artificial orchids. Windows filled the living room walls, allowing natural light to fill the room.

With an open concept, a small kitchen with an island stood to the left. Stainless steel appliances littering the cabinets and granite countertops made the meaning behind Stanley's comments obvious when he said the Society was generous. The room looked as if it had been duplicated from a magazine.

All at once, I heard a female voice to my left. A figure suddenly appeared from the hallway next to the kitchen leading to the back part of the flat. She looked as if she could be of Native American descent with dark eyes, high cheek bones, beautiful tanned skin, and a long black braid down her back.

Confidently she stood near the granite countertop, studying me from head to toe.

Looks like I have a new roommate. I can take it from here, Stanley.

Stanley seemed amused by the small girl's confidence. Grinning, he nodded and shut the door behind him. I returned my gaze back to the girl by the counter. She sprang into action as soon as my guide's footsteps grew silent.

My name is Kate. It's nice to meet you....

Darcy.

Darcy. Well, let me show you around the place. Of course, this is the living room and kitchen area. In the back are two bedrooms and a bathroom. Mine is on the left and yours is on the right.

She waved her hand emphatically and started walking back toward the hallway. Opening the door to her room, clothes were scattered on the bed and floor. Though her bedcovers were wadded in a mound in the middle of her bed, I could tell that the Society had decorated every room in the flat with great skill and opulence.

Sorry it's such a mess. I'm not a fan of folding laundry or making the bed. But don't worry, I clean up after myself around the flat. Here, let's see your room.

Crossing the hall, she opened the door parallel to hers. The room was identical to hers, minus the clothes and unmade bed.

Hardwood floors, creamy walls, and white bedding provided the upscale country elegance that the rest of the flat embodied. Unlike Kate's room, mine held a large window overlooking the desert. The natural light streaming in through the glass clung to the wispy curtains surrounding the bed. It was Kate who broke the silence, luckily before my jaw dropped.

I guess they feel like spoiling us makes up for kidnapping us from our homes.

Turning toward her, I saw that Kate had a small smirk across her face. I couldn't help but notice our similar opinion of our "recruitment." She shrugged her shoulder as if dismissing my concern.

Eh, we can't talk like that here though. One of the cult members will lecture you on the goodness of the Society.

Do they kidnap every recruit?

Most of them. Some of them have parents who have been in the Society since its creation. The ones who aren't related are taken from their homes. All people who have no one to care about them, miss them after they're gone.

You don't have anyone?

My family lives on a reservation in South Dakota. Very traditional. Too traditional to be open-minded about the "pale skin" I fell in love with. So, they exiled me. Shortly after, my boyfriend decided he'd be better off with Miss Cheerleader who had a rich daddy. The guy I lost everything for left me without a second glance.

Her dark eyes had turned glossy and seemed to be looking off into the distance with soured memories.

I'm so sorry.

Breaking away from her focus on the horizon outside the window, her face brightened as she smiled and wiped a stray tear away.

Not your fault. I was stupid. But since you're here, that means you don't have anyone back home either? No parents, siblings, boyfriend?

My chest tightened in silent anguish as the pain flooded back to my mind, out of the cage in the back of my brain where I shoved my grief. It was obvious she saw me wince at her questions. She apologetically put her hands up and took a step back.

Sorry, didn't mean to pry.

No, no. You're fine. My father died eighteen years ago and my mother died several months ago. No brothers or sisters.

She nodded and pursed her lips, understanding that no more detail was needed than that.

Well, what a way to start a friendship. Bear our souls to the point of discomfort. You hungry?

Starving.

I think we have some food in the kitchen. They restock us weekly but since I've been the only tenant in this apartment for a couple weeks, they've only been giving enough for me. Tomorrow should bring a new shipment of food.

So, they don't serve us gruel from a sketchy cafeteria then? She laughed and motioned for me to follow her to the kitchen.

Oh, no. They just stock our rooms and don't bother with a cafeteria. Reduces the waste of cooking in bulk and having to pay cooks.

She opened the fridge and stood looking at its contents. Her long braid nearly touched the small of her back. Kate wore an army green tank top and jean shorts with frayed edges. Though she was quite beautiful, she also held a tomboyish charm about her. The perfect example of a strong woman, she embodied both confident toughness and femininity.

Ummmm... well we have eggs and bread. Care for breakfast for lunch?

Sounds delicious. I'm starving.

How do you like your eggs?

Scrambled is fine. Thanks.

Over the next twenty minutes, Kate casually fixed lunch. She had a gracefulness about her every move, making her simple task of scrambling eggs seem like artwork. As she sat the plate of toast and eggs in front of me at the island where I sat watching her, the scent of the breakfast caused my stomach to churn. It seemed

24

like an eternity since I had eaten the packets of crackers in the medical unit.

Kate and I sat on the stools next to the island, eating and talking about what life was like in the Society. She had only been here a couple of weeks. The normal schedule consisted of morning training sessions from seven in the morning until noon. Morning classes included courses like self-defense, fitness workouts, and weapons practice.

Trainees are then released to shower and eat lunch. Then, the afternoon session begins at two and ends at six. Afternoon classes consisted of more academic topics: language, etiquette, and culture topics. Basic school subjects are mixed within the three aforementioned topics including math, chemistry, history, and English.

Looking at the digital time on the stove, it read eleven o'clock.

So why aren't you in your morning training now?

Oh, they excused me from it to greet and introduce you to the flat. I have you to thank for missing out on kickboxing today.

She patted me on the shoulder and laughed as she picked up the empty dishes from the counter, setting them in the sink. Rubbing her hands together, she displayed an ornery grin and looked at me still sitting at the counter.

Now, it's time for the real tour. But first, we need to get you changed.

I looked down at the t-shirt and sweats they had given me at the medical unit. When I looked up, I saw Kate's back as she hurried down the hall toward the bedrooms. I found her in my room, rummaging through the closet and drawers.

So, what do you like to wear? They supply us with a variety of clothes from basic tees and tanks to dresses and heels.

How do they know what size to buy for everyone?

They size you before you regain consciousness in your hospital room. My clothes were ready for me when I got to the flat too.

Wow. Another beautiful example of the privacy they provide to us here in the "cult."

One thing that can be said about the Society is they are always five steps ahead of you.

I paused before walking toward where she was bent over the bottom drawer of the dresser. Not bothering to look through the entire stock of clothes they provided, I grabbed a blue tank top and a pair of dark blue jean shorts. Kate nodded her head and walked out the bedroom door.

I'll meet you in the living room. I'm going to freshen up before we go.

As soon as the door shut, I shed my sweats and stepped into the shorts. Kate wasn't kidding when she said they measured our sizes. The shorts fit like I had bought them myself in the store. I pulled the t-shirt over my head and revealed the sports bra that I had been wearing when I was taken.

Surely, they provided underwear. I shuffled through the top drawers in the dresser, finding a whole drawer of bras and underwear. Lace and silk overflowed over the top of the drawer. I chose a standard pink cotton bra from the top and ditched the sports bra.

The hallway was quiet as I went in search of the bathroom. Ever since I had thrown up, I'd been wanting to brush my teeth and wash my face. The bathroom was at the end of the hall. A double vanity, jacuzzi bath, and shower with frosted glass filled the bathroom.

Although all the walls in the flat were painted the same color, the bathroom had an accent wall with barn wood covering the entire surface. The mirror extended the length of the vanity and the toilet sat against the furthest wall. My sandals smacked loudly against the tile floor which had a natural stone appearance.

I hurried to the vanity and opened the cabinets beneath the sink. There I found washcloths and toothbrushes, one of which was already labeled with Kate's name. Running the rag under warm water, I placed my face over the sink and rubbed the soaking cloth over my grimy face. The heat of the water was refreshing and cleansing.

Looking in the mirror at my reflection, I quickly scanned over my hastily chosen outfit. The outline of my slender yet delicately curved body, nearly an exact copy of my mother, could be seen beneath the fitting clothing I had chosen. I dried the water from my face and retrieved my assigned toothbrush. After brushing my teeth, I exited the bathroom and walked toward the other end of the flat.

Kate was sprawled across the couch, manipulating the woven material of one of the throw blankets. When she saw me, she jumped up and headed for the door.

Let the real tour begin. If we hurry, we might be able to see someone get kicked in the face.

The sound of her chuckle filled the hallway as we locked the door behind us. We walked toward a set of elevators past several other flats. Kate pressed the first-floor button immediately and leaned against the wall.

The first floor is for the nurses, educational staff, and executive guards like Stanley. The second floor is for the training guards. They are the ones who oversee the recruits and train them in the morning sessions. The third, fourth, and fifth floors are for the recruits. The flats are quite large so it's not nearly as many recruits as you may think. Maybe thirty or forty of us all together. They rotate them out so fast, the number stays low. They probably like it that way so no rebellion can take place.

Rebellion? I was told the recruits tend to change their minds about this place after several weeks.

One of the brainwashed ones must have told you that. Most of the recruits fall for the line that they feed us but there's a small number of us that merely tolerate their teachings in hope of getting out of here.

But they put tracking devices in us. Aren't you worried that if you ran off after deployment that they would find you?

Nothing a sharp knife and a little blood can't fix.

A chill traveled down my spine just as the elevator doors opened. Kate made a zipping gesture over her mouth before leaving the confines of the elevator. I followed her through the same hall that Stanley and I had taken to get to the flat. However, instead of continuing straight, Kate turned down a hall to the right.

Kate explained that this hall took us to the training gyms and to the classrooms. She pointed out several rooms with desks lined in rows as well as a personal gym filled with treadmills, ellipticals, and small weights.

Near the end of the hall, two sets of double doors stood parallel to one another. Kate opened the set of doors on the left and flipped the light switch just inside the door. The room lit up under florescent lights, revealing countless weapons: guns, knives, archery bows, and bow staffs.

This is the weapons room. We usually start in the other gym and end up here before lunch. Who needs coffee when you have the sound of gunshots to wake you up first thing in the morning?

As we started walking back to the gym entrance, my eyes glossed over the countless weapons that filled the glass cases. For such a peaceful society, they sure had a lot of violence on display.

Come on. I don't want to miss the fights.

Kate had already reached the double doors and stood waiting for me to follow. There was no impatience in her tone toward me, only excitement for the possible entertainment. I hurried over to the doors and flipped the light switch behind me.

Once again back in the hall, Kate rushed over to the double doors parallel to the weapons room. She pushed the right door open and grabbed my hand, pulling me through the entrance.

Inside the doors, a giant room stood before us. There were various stations placed around the room with a running track around its circumference. Inside the track, a boxing ring, wrestling matts, and gym equipment littered the center of the room.

Around the boxing ring, stood dozens of recruits. They all wore fitness apparel and seemed to have been sweating for some time now. The recruits themselves comprised a wide range of races and heights, mostly female and a good third of them male.

Inside the ring stood two men. Both men reaching at least six feet tall faced each other and hopped on their feet. One of the men had blonde hair cut high and tight, was slightly shorter than the other, and held a sort of arrogance in his posture. He was slightly stockier than the other, puffing his chest out rather flamboyantly.

His opponent was nearly the exact opposite of him: slimmer yet still muscular, dark hair, and cautious demeanor. My curiosity had distracted me from the door which now slammed behind us. Some of the recruits glanced our way quickly but seemed captivated by the fight in front of them, returning their gaze to the competitors.

The tall, dark-featured man had been instructing them on dos and don'ts of hand-to-hand combat. As we walked up and stood behind the other recruits, his eyes caught our arrival. They scanned over Kate, most likely familiar to him already, but settled on me.

My chest fluttered as his eyes focused on me. Closer, I could tell that he was a very attractive man. His jawline could cut glass, his arms showed dips and curves from bulging muscles, and his eyes held a certain intensity that could make any girl swoon.

It was in that brief moment that his opponent took the opportunity to kick him right across the face. The handsome fighter was stunned for a moment while his competitor reveled in his victorious hit.

And that, recruits, is why you never let yourself get distracted.

But the once-stunned fighter did not stay that way for long. He punched his cocky companion straight in the face. The blonde slumped over and grabbed his nose. Standing up, blood could be seen coming through his hands.

And that is also why you never get cocky before the fight is over. That's it for today, recruits. You are now free to return to your flats before the afternoon lessons begin.

The recruits filed out of the gym, leaving behind the two fighters. The blonde glared with his hands still over his nose before retreating from the boxing ring, leaving his opponent alone.

Kate nudged me on the arm and nodded her head toward the door. The last of the recruits and the bloodied fighter had let the door shut behind them. I followed Kate back toward the exit but couldn't help but glance back at the handsome victor.

Much to my surprise, he stood in the center of the ring looking right back at me. I hurriedly returned my gaze to the back of Kate as we reached the exit doors. Back in the hall, my heart returned to its normal speed.

Well, that's the end of the tour. Let's go back to the flat before classes.

I nodded in agreement, with the vision of intense eyes still haunting my thoughts.

IV.

THE GUARDS

Once back in the loft, Kate and I both claimed a couch in the living room and sprawled across the numerous pillows and blankets.

So, what did you think?

The gyms are enormous, and the classrooms remind me of high school.

And much like high school, you are forced against your will to take stupid classes.

We both gazed off in the distance, perhaps remembering the days of our high school careers. Life was so much simpler back then. It wasn't long before the intense eyes once again returned to the forefront of my mind.

So, who were those guys fighting in the ring?

The arrogant, blonde douchebag is Connor. He's the typical hard-headed jock who thinks he owns everything and everyone.

Yeah, he seemed pretty cocky.

The other one is Ben. He is the head of the training guards, which is another reason why Connor felt the need to show off. He hates that Ben ranks above him.

How does Ben feel about Connor?

*Well, he tolerates him better than a lot of other guards do…
but that can also just be Ben's demeanor. He is always so stoic.
He's super talented but also ridiculously hard on himself.*

I nodded in understanding, absorbing all the information.
She seemed to read my curiosity, her eyes twinkling as she grinned
at me.

The guards are quite handsome, aren't they?

*Yes, they are. Although this place is not necessarily the
most romantic place to have that kind of thing in mind, right?*

*You'd be surprised. You see, what the Board and President
don't know is that the guards all have their own set of rules. If
they do know, they merely sweep it under the rug to please their
guards. One of the guards' rules is that they get to claim their own
recruits.*

What do you mean claim?

*Some of the guards participate in claiming female recruits
as their "evening entertainment." As recruits, there is nothing that
we can do. It's a horrible practice but it's not the first time we
don't get a say in something. Anyways, not all of the guards
participate and most of the recruits never get claimed.*

The disgust must have been apparent on my face because
Kate looked down at her hands folded in her lap.

All recruits have a grace period of three weeks before they can get claimed. After that, you're fair game. My third week mark is in two days.

She lifted her face, her eyes filled with worry. Sympathy washed over me as I watched the small girl rub her hands together over and over again. I stood up and walked to where she sat, plopping down beside her.

Hey, like you said it doesn't happen to everyone. And over my dead body will some douchebag come in here to claim you as his property.

She nodded her head, though she didn't seem convinced. At that point, my eyes began to get heavy and the rest of the energy drained out of my body. Kate seemed to register this fact and patted my back.

Go take a nap. You look like you're about to pass out. I'll wake you up before classes.

Thanks, Kate.

I retreated to my room and collapsed onto my bed. The comforter was soft and the sheer curtains relaxing. The warmth of the afternoon sun coming through my window made falling asleep instantaneous.

The smell of popcorn filled the air as the kernels popped loudly in the microwave. My mom, always humming in the kitchen, was getting sodas and popcorn ready for our movie night.

35

We made it one of our rituals every Friday night. Cuddled under most of the blankets in the house, we would eat popcorn and laugh together.

Visions of my mother fill my head. Her soft brown hair pulled into a messy bun on the back of her head. I could hear her laugh again. It was the kind of laugh that was infectious, a beautiful sound that seemed to come from the sincerest depth of her soul.

I moved closer to her under the blanket, desiring to feel the security of her arms again. Her laugh still filled the air; her sweet flowery scent filled my lungs. Her hand rubbed my back and her chin lay on the top of my head.

But I am holding her too tight. If I let go of her, she'll be gone forever. Much to my chagrin, she begins to wiggle from my grasp. With understanding and loving eyes, she looks down at me.

You can't hold onto me forever. That's no way to live.

And then I am awake. My eyes fly open. I am hugging a pillow to my chest as the ache inside my heart threatens to burst. Sitting up abruptly, I find myself desperately searching for my mom. Reality hits hard as my eyes find white sheets, wood floors, and the endless desert horizon outside of my window.

Suddenly, a soft knock resounds through the room.

Darcy, it's almost time for afternoon classes. We don't want to be late.

Coming.

Throwing the sandals that I had chosen earlier back onto my feet, I opened the door and walked toward the kitchen. Kate stood by the door, books and pencils in hand. Handing me one set, we made our way back down to the classrooms. Kate had a certain giddiness as she guided me down the hallway.

The classroom where we sat held rows of tables facing a whiteboard. Other recruits were already settled while some still filed in the door and found their seats.

Suddenly, the room was quiet as a solid looking African American man walked through the door. The unseated recruits found their desks immediately and the remainder of the class grew very still and attentive.

The man was young and attractive, skin a beautiful dark caramel color and eyes a soft brown. Immediately, I noticed the kindness of his eyes and the humble way he carried himself. He had reached the front of the room at this point, laying the books in his hands on the front desk facing the class.

He was definitely not what I expected in an educator. My mind filled with visions of a middle-aged man with glasses low on the brim of his nose. Being not more than twenty-five, this man seemed out of place with students so seemingly close to his own age.

I could feel the energy coming from Kate. Ironically, she seemed both jittery and stiff, sitting straight as a rod and yet unable to keep the pencil in her hand still for very long.

Realizing that I was studying her nervous behavior, her eyes met mine and her pencil ceased movement. Blood rushed to her cheeks and a slight grin spread across her face before her gaze returned to the handsome teacher at the front of the room.

I couldn't help but smile as I witnessed my new friend go from confident to a fluttery ball of anxiety. It was at this point in my entertainment of Kate that the teacher cleared his throat.

For those recruits who have just joined us, my name is Noah Fletcher. I teach various courses here at this facility including business, history, and martial arts. Today, we will be covering the topic of business. Particularly, today's topic will cover some of the institutions that make businesses succeed or fail.

Mr. Fletcher walked behind the podium and rifled through a basket in its cabinet, pulling out a marker. He walked to the dry erase board and turned back toward his audience.

Many of your field assignments after your training is complete will relate to business in one form or another. Whether you are placed in the White House or in a grade school, your business acumen will come in handy at some point in your career. So, can anyone tell me foundational items that a business needs to succeed?

The classroom was utterly silent for the first few moments after his question. A girl with fiery red curls draped down her back raised her hand first.

Money.

Ah, yes. Where else to begin but the thing that allows a business to begin and succeed but kills it in its absence. What else?

A husky Latin American man near the front of the class stated that leadership is what directs the business. Seeming pleased with this answer, Noah added it to the board under money. Various other answers were given throughout the rest of the class including manpower, communication, and information. The time went by quickly as the teacher intelligently interacted with his students.

After nearly an hour and a half, the teacher closed his book and dismissed the students to attend their next class. Kate motioned for me to wait for her as she stood up. Hesitating first, she finally seemed to get the nerve to approach the teacher.

As he turned toward her, I could see in his eyes that he was just as excited to see her as she was to see him. His brown eyes, though soft before, seemed to utterly melt into her as they spoke. Their body language displayed a nervous delight as the two seemed helplessly drawn to one another. While she walked away, his gaze on her remained unbroken.

And not the type of look from a guy that made you feel like a repulsed piece of meat. It wasn't the lustful, checking-out-her-butt-while-she-walks-away kind of look but one that revealed their inescapable magnetism for one another.

When we reached the hallway again, I grabbed a hold of Kate's arm and pulled her toward me excitedly.

What was that about?

I don't know what you're talking about.

You totally have a crush on the teacher!

I do not. Like you said, this isn't exactly the type of place that people fall in love, Darcy.

Though her statement was true, there was just something perfect about the two of them that seemed to surpass their circumstances.

You don't know that. People have fallen in love in war, poverty, famine, and in an age where texting is the only form of communication.

We laughed into our next classroom where a stern woman sat at the teacher's desk at the front of the room. Her look of disappointment and stern demeanor was a heavy dampener on my previous humor and made for a long class period.

Three classes each an hour and twenty minutes long concluded the day's lessons. Kate introduced me to some of the other recruits between classes. Though they were all friendly, everyone seemed to avoid talking about our involuntary recruitment into the Society. Many of them actually seemed happy with their forced lifestyle.

After the lessons were done, Kate and I returned to our flat and ate peanut butter sandwiches for dinner. Taking turns in the shower, we both went our separate ways for the night.

When came time for my shower, I couldn't get in quick enough. The hot water felt like it washed away a lifetime of grime. Standing under the stream, the hot water poured through my hair and down my back and arms. The mirror in the bathroom was covered in condensation when I finally stepped out of the shower.

The towel that I wrapped around my body was warm and soft. As I made my way back to my room, the air was cool on my skin. Slipping into a cotton t-shirt and shorts, I crawled under the inviting comforter and collapsed, utterly exhausted from the day.

So much had changed in such a short amount of time. It felt like a week had passed since I first woke up in the medical unit with Evelyn. Amazingly, I made a new friend and learned more than I would have in a whole week of public school.

Yet, the reality of where I was and how I got there remained a heavy burden in my thoughts. Visions of Margot's stoic face haunted my thoughts as my eyes grew heavy. Restlessly, I tossed and turned the entire night with images of veteran's memorials, gray pant suits, and bloody noses intruding my dreams. It was only when the vision of dark hair and intense eyes filled my thoughts that I slept peacefully for however short of time.

V.

TIMBER

The next morning, I woke up to Kate knocking on my door. The clock beside my bed read six-thirty in the morning. Morning lessons started in thirty minutes.

Don't forget we have class soon. Wear something comfortable. We have self-defense classes today.

I jumped up out of bed and threw on workout clothes, gray jogging capris and an aquamarine racerback top. Slipping on tennis shoes and throwing my hair in a ponytail, I opened the door and hurried toward the kitchen.

A bowl sat on the middle of the island with an assortment of fruit as well as boxes of cereal and a gallon of milk. Kate sat at the counter with a bowl of cereal, sliced banana littering its contents.

Morning. They stocked the kitchen this morning. There's fruit and cereal. If you don't want any of this, the fridge is full of food.

Cereal is fine.

I sat down next to her and grabbed the empty bowl she had placed there, filling it with cereal and milk. She pushed the other half of her unused banana toward me and I helped myself to the slices, adding them to my own cereal.

Putting the bowls into the sink, we left the flat and headed toward the gym. Several recruits were scattered across the wrestling mats, conversing with one another while they sat on the firm vinyl.

Kate chose a seat next to some other recruits and tapped the mat next to her, inviting me to join their circle. Within the group was the redhead from the day before with her hair braided down her back, several curls loose around her face. Other members of our group included a lanky African American girl and a man that looked to be in his late twenties with a cut-off displaying his wiry muscles.

After ten minutes of loitering the mats, the gym door slammed shut behind a pair of guards. They were the same pair from the previous day who bloodied one another boxing. As always, the blonde held an air of arrogance as he strutted across the gym floor.

My heart fluttered as my eyes reached the other guard. As he drew closer, the green of his eyes became more and more apparent. Wearing athletic shorts and a t-shirt, Ben stood tall compared to most of the recruits who had gotten to their feet upon the guards' arrival.

They eventually walked past my group. Much to my surprise, Connor was the one to acknowledge my presence.

Originally glancing through the entire group of recruits, his eyes stayed on me. He arrived at my side and towered over me, looking down at me like a cat over a mouse.

Looks like we got a new recruit. Let me know when your three weeks are up, darlin'.

His hot breath landed on the side of my face as I stood frozen in place. A shiver went down my back as I attempted to hold down the cereal I had just eaten.

Connor, enough. Class needs to begin.

Ben had gone to the front of the group but still stood waiting for his companion to join him. Connor smirked and gave my body one more thorough inspection before returning to Ben's side. I chanced a look at Ben, attempting to thank him for his interruption. However, his eyes merely glanced over me before he began to address the recruits.

Today, we are going to begin with our fitness course before we move onto self-defense. Get your muscles warmed up before the lesson. You know what to do. Ten laps around the gym, fifty push-ups, one hundred sit-ups. Then, I'll have instructions.

The recruits all began jogging around the circumference of the gym while the guards stood supervising. Connor faced Ben, probably making some kind of crude joke. Though he seemed to please himself in his "professional" humor, Ben seemed to otherwise ignore his partner and watched the recruits run their laps.

My chest grew tight as I approached where they stood. I didn't know whether it was from the fear that Connor would become aware of my approach or the fact that Ben was observing every person who passed him. Kate ran alongside me, keeping up with my lengthier legs easily.

Connor's a pig. Just ignore him. He'll eventually lose interest by the time three weeks have gone by.

Her reassurance did anything but calm my fears. Connor didn't seem like the kind that gave up or lost interest in the hunt. As we ran by, Ben followed our trail with his deep green eyes. Up close, he was even more handsome than I had noticed the day before.

His skin seemed somehow tanned which made the chiseled muscles of his arms even more appealing to the eyes. His dark brown hair, having grown since his last cut, curled a little on the ends near his face. With a strong jawline, intense eyes, and towering height, Ben was attractive to say the very least.

His eyes lingered on us for only a second before more recruits ran past where he stood. After finishing their running and exercises, every recruit was glistening with perspiration. Ben called attention to the front of the class where he demonstrated with Connor various blocking techniques.

While Connor was out to show off, Ben seemed to genuinely want the recruits to learn. He was passionate and informative, commanding the room with his knowledge and presence. After the demonstration, the recruits paired off together to practice their own blocking.

The guards walked around and coached the recruits, correcting their form or praising their progress. Of course, Kate and I chose each other to be partners. Though she was inches shorter than me, she made it known that she could hold her own. Quick and strong, Kate proved to be a worthy opponent despite her small stature.

As a beginner, I was not at the level that Kate performed. However, I had always been a quick learner and athletic in almost any sport I attempted. In high school gym class, I was known to embarrass a couple of cocky boys from time to time.

It was then that Connor interrupted my thoughts. Suddenly, I felt his presence right behind me, uncomfortably close.

Your form could use some adjustment. Let me help you.

I felt his hands on my shoulders, lowering my arms slightly. He kicked his foot between mine to widen my stance. His touch was enough to make me want another shower.

There you go. Now let's see how quick you can move.

He gestured for Kate to step away with a dismissive wave of the hand before placing himself square in front of me. Hesitating for only a second, Connor began striking toward me, building speed as I successfully blocked his advances.

He seemed to be feeding off my success, driven to make me miss one. The speed became more than I could keep up with.

Suddenly, the wind was knocked out of my lungs as one of his blows struck me square in the chest. My legs went out from beneath me and I landed on my butt on the gym mat.

Connor smirked down at me in triumph while I still sat stunned by the blow. His hits weren't necessarily meant for beginners first learning to block.

Enough. Connor, move along.

The voice was deep and right behind me. Whatever breath I had regained was sucked straight out of me. It was Ben, and Connor did not seem pleased with his arrival.

Ben, how do you expect them to learn if you aren't hard on them?

It's her first day, Connor, and you weren't holding your punches. Move along.

At first, Connor remained standing over me. It wasn't until Ben placed himself between us with his back to Connor that he arrogantly shrugged it off and walked away, probably going to pick on another recruit.

I looked up to see Ben holding out his hand to help me up from the ground. Hesitantly, I placed my hand in his seemingly larger one and was pulled back to my feet. Electricity ran up my arm as his warmth spread from my hand. He released it almost immediately and watched me dust myself off.

You okay?

Yes, just a little winded.

You're new here but I think I saw you yesterday. I'm Ben Lewis.

Darcy Bishop.

Well, Darcy, welcome. If you are sure you're okay, please rejoin Kate in practice.

I nodded my head and walked to where Kate was standing and watching. Her eyes were wide in shock.

Darcy! Are you okay? He totally walloped you in the chest.

I'm fine, thanks.

You're lucky Ben came when he did. I don't think Connor knows when to stop. He once bloodied a recruit's nose before another guard stepped in. I didn't even know Ben knew my name! He's always so serious and professional.

After Kate rambled on for a moment, we returned to our practice. It was a relief to be up against Kate again and not in actual danger of taking a punch to the face. Even when Kate outhit me, she had the respect to pull her punches.

After the first hour and a half of class, Ben allowed the recruits to get a drink of water before the next lesson. Looking around the gym, I noticed Connor heading toward the gym doors. However, before he reached them, Noah entered through the heavy double doors. They nodded to one other in respect as they passed through the opening simultaneously.

Kate was immediately aware that Noah had arrived and returned back to the state of jittery nervousness as the day before.

I thought Noah taught the afternoon lessons.

He does. But he helps Ben with martial arts every once in a while. He's really good.

As Noah approached Ben, a smile spread across their faces. Clasping hands, the two seemed to be quite close to one another. Noah took off his jacket, leaving on a white cutoff and gray jogging pants. Without sleeves, it was obvious that Noah lifted weights often by the size of his arms and chest.

He was several inches shorter than Ben but was a stockier build. The two seemed to be relieved that Connor was not joining them. In fact, the entire atmosphere of the gym changed once Connor left. The recruits seemed happier and actually able to enjoy themselves in physical activity without the fear of abuse.

Noah called attention to the class with Ben by his side.

For this lesson, recruits, we will actually be journeying across the hall. We will be learning how to properly handle bow staffs today.

Many of the students seemed excited upon hearing his announcement. Picking up their jackets and bottles of water, everyone made their way across the hall to the weapons gymnasium. Bow staffs were dispersed, and recruits remained paired off.

Ben and Noah walked us through the basics of how to hold, stand, and advance with the bow staff.

In the end, you should be quite agile with the bow staff.

Noah met eye contact with Ben who nodded in approval. Suddenly, Noah burst into action, advancing quickly on Ben. Ben blocked his advancement and the two sparred with one another rapidly. The sparring ended just as suddenly as it stopped with both competitors grinning from ear to ear. It was obvious that the two enjoyed being together with even intense fights ending in comradery.

Partners began sparring once the demonstration was over. With the bow staff being nearly the height of Kate, she struggled a little more with this activity than the last. Noah walked by and noticed the difficulty she faced. He grinned slightly at the sight of the small girl attempting to handle the long stick stealthily.

Here, let me help you.

Kate blushed when she realized that Noah had been watching her. He approached her slowly and corrected her grasp on the staff. Reaching for my staff, Noah nodded his head in appreciation as I handed it to him.

So, if I come at you like this, you should block it horizontally. Yes, like that.

Even practice sparring, the two seemed totally infatuated with one another. It was obvious that Noah was taking it easy on her as he coached her step by step. After a few minutes, Noah surrendered the staff back to me. However, he turned his attention back to Kate before moving onto the next pair of recruits.

Before I go, you've been here three weeks, right?

Fear filled Kate's eyes as Noah awkwardly stood there waiting for her reply. Her face went pale and her mouth hung open. He seemed to suddenly become aware of how she interpreted his question.

Oh, no. Not like that. I was just wondering if you wanted to hang out tonight. No expectations, just talking. Midnight marks your three weeks and I just didn't want you to be claimed like a piece of meat.

Relief flooded over Kate before the blood rushed back to her cheeks. She grinned up at Noah and nodded in agreement.

Okay, I'll see you then.

As soon as Noah walked away, I ran over to Kate's side. I couldn't help but smile as Kate stood in awe of what happened.

I knew it. You guys are so crazy about each other!

I don't know what you're talking about.

Oh, please. Leave some blood for the rest of your body, cheeks.

We both laughed as Kate rubbed her cheeks with her hands before we continued sparring with our bow staffs. Every once in a while, I could see Noah and Kate steal glances toward each other.

Though they seemed perfect together, I couldn't help but wonder what would happen when she was assigned to the field and he stayed behind. There was no happily ever after here. Only the control of the Society. And I had a feeling love wasn't one of their top priorities.

The day went by quickly as we finished our morning lessons, showered, ate lunch, and went to our afternoon classes. Today's first lecture was on the topic of government. The three branches of the government were covered as well as the checks and balances needed for each branch to have the same regulated power.

Before long, Kate and I found ourselves back at the flat. For dinner, I offered to fix my mom's famous parmesan chicken accompanied with salad and garlic mashed potatoes. The entire apartment flooded with the smell of parmesan and herbs as I opened the oven door.

Kate eagerly watched as I plated each of our dinners. I rounded the corner of the island and set the plates down before us. As I chewed my first bite of chicken, memories of my mother flooded into my mind.

The kitchen in our house was small but daintily decorated. The cabinets were painted white with scalloped edges and the walls were a pastel yellow. At the time, I was around eight years old. I had always loved helping my mom fix dinner after school.

It was late spring, a cool breeze rustling the lace curtains around the open window. The birds were chirping outside and the windchime jingled softly in the distance. The sun was still above the horizon, casting shadows on the front porch steps.

Next to the counter, I stood on one of the chairs from the dining room. My mother had her hands in the breading, patting the chicken into the parmesan crumbs before placing it in the pan for the oven. She was one of the most patient people I've ever known, not becoming irritated as my young hands made messes in the kitchen.

She taught me all the things growing up that she believed a mother should: sowing, cleaning, cooking, modesty, and strength. Her wisdom was beyond her years. She was a constant companion to me through triumphs and hardships. In the end, I didn't only lose my mother, I lost a friend, advisor, and confidant.

This chicken is delicious.

Thanks, it was my mother's recipe. She wouldn't give her secret to anyone else but me.

Kate just smiled. I could tell that she was thinking about her own mother. Her smile faded and so did that topic of conversation. We went on to lighter topics as we finished our dinner. Since I had cooked the meal, Kate offered to do the dishes while I cleaned up for bed.

Thanks, Kate. I hope you enjoy your date tonight.
It's not a date!
Mmhmm.

I smiled at her and retreated toward my bedroom before she could deny the obvious anymore. Later that night, I heard a knock at the door. Peeking out of my bedroom door, I watched as Noah came through the door and the couple went to the couch to talk. I quietly shut my door so as to not bother them.

My dreams were restless yet again that night. Images of Connor fighting me haunted my thoughts. He relentlessly knocked me down, taking the breath from my lungs. Each time that I would stand up, a hard blow would be delivered to my chest. I woke up in a fit, gasping for breath. Sweat had gathered on my temples and my shirt clung to my back. I looked over at the clock next to my bed and saw that it was two in the morning.

Putting my bare feet on the cool floor, I made my way to the kitchen for a drink of water. As I rounded the corner, I was stopped dead in my tracks. Kate and Noah were still on the couch talking. Kate held one of the throw blankets in her lap and Noah sat with his feet on the coffee table. They both looked up at me as I came into view.

I am so sorry. I had no idea you were still up.

It's fine, Darcy. What are you doing up?

Um, just needed some water.

I walked to the cabinet and filled the first glass I found with cool tap water from the sink. Giving Kate an apologetic look, I made my way back to my room. Before I rounded the corner, I saw the look on Kate's face as she returned to her conversation with Noah. Her eyes sparkled above the love drunk grin that brightened her entire expression. It was the face of someone falling in love, falling hard.

VI.

THREE WEEKS' NOTICE

The next three weeks seemed to pass at a brisk rate. The days were filled with lessons. In the morning, Ben would teach courses varying from self-defense and boxing to weapons training and stealth. With each lesson, my skills improved to the point that I felt confident against other recruits. Afternoon lessons seemed to linger with the topics being strictly academic. Not only that, but some of the older teachers were rather harsh and monotonous.

Kate claimed that one of the teachers, a gray-haired and rather stern woman, had a ruler in her desk that she used to spank unruly recruits. I knew that she was joking but I could not stop a laugh from slipping on one occasion. The female instructor had just corrected a student's wrong answer, frowning, when she opened up one of her desk drawers.

Out of the drawer, she pulled out a wooden ruler slowly. Before I realized it, I had let out a laugh and drawn the attention of the entire class. I glanced over at Kate who was looking down at her textbook, struggling to control herself. Looking back toward the teacher, I received a cold look.

I am so sorry. Please continue, ma'am.

Thank you for both your interruption and your permission to continue with the lesson.

Her obvious sarcasm sobered my attitude as she turned toward the dry erase board to continue her lecture with the ruler. Totally shocked by the encounter, I turned to Kate who was still struggling to contain her laughter. Her lips twitched and her hands were gripped hard against the textbook, her knuckles white with the pressure. I just smiled and shook my head, returning my attention to the equation at hand.

After the first couple weeks, I felt like I was fitting in with the other recruits. I had made a handful of good friends with whom I shared most of my classes and become accustomed to the Society's schedule. Remembering what Stanley had said about recruits' change of heart after the first couple weeks made sense now.

It was after this period of time that recruits began to forget the outside world and get lost in their lessons and new friends. However, in the back of my mind, I still held my suspicions of the Society and their President, Margot Clarke.

At the beginning of my third week at the facility, Ben and Connor led yet another class in self-defense. However, today held more tension than other days. Connor seemed especially aggressive toward the recruits. He was excessively handsy and involved in the practice sparring. Many of them merely ignored him or tolerated his pestering.

It was inevitable that he would eventually approach my partner and me. Kate and I had decided to switch it up that day and partner with a couple of our other friends: Kate with the red-head, Hannah, and me with Brendan, a lanky boy who preferred computer classes.

Connor immediately turned his attention on me rather than Brendan, who backed away slowly as he approached. Ben had been called out of the gym for a moment by another guard which only encouraged Connor's behavior.

Let's see how much you've improved, champ.

He stepped into place in front of me and put up his fists. I lowered my hands and took a step back.

I don't have anything to prove to you, Connor. Just let me practice with Brendan.

At that point, the recruits had all ceased practice and were watching the event unfold. Connor did not seem to acknowledge my rejection of him in the slightest and continued to advance toward me.

Connor. I'm serious.

Suddenly, he sprang into action, jabbing both fists toward me in rapid motion. I blocked every advancement he attempted and stepped out of the way of his body as he lunged in my direction. He stumbled forwards before regaining his step and faced me once again.

This time, Connor came at me with full force with his strikes increasing in speed and power. Blocking his punches began to hurt my arms and I struggled to block every swing. Adrenaline rushed through my veins as I realized he was totally out of control. Instinct kicked in as I saw an opening between his broad swings, landing a solid punch square on the nose.

His shock was almost as instantaneous as the blood pouring from his nose. Yet, his astonishment did not last long as rage immediately spread across his face. Before he could lunge toward me, another figure dove in between us and knocked Connor to the ground.

Ben pinned him to the ground as Connor attempted to roll, pounding his arms on the gym mat. The sound of his arms thrashing against the mat filled the entire gymnasium in loud surges.

That's enough, Connor. You need to go.

Get off of me! That little brat needs to be taught a lesson.

Ben remained on Connor as he continued his struggle to fight me, tension coursing through his body. He reached to his side where a beeper was placed on his waistband, pressing a button. Within a minute, Noah and another guard ran into the gym. Seeing Ben on top of Connor, they rushed to their leader's aid. With a guard on each arm, Connor was picked up from the ground and taken out of the gym.

On the entire way out, he glared in my direction, blood dripping down his mouth. His eyes were focused on me with a look of determination, a gruesome sight as the blood covered his toothy grin.

Now free from his troublesome partner, Ben ran his hands through his hair and turned his back to the recruits. When he spun back around, his pupils were dilated from the adrenaline and the green of his irises had darkened.

You are dismissed for a water break. Meet back in the weapons room.

The recruits gathered their things and filed out the doors quietly, aware of Ben's frustration. Kate's face was full of concern as she waited for me to join her side.

Darcy, stay.

Ben's voice had calmed as he stood watching the rest of the recruits leave. I shot Kate an apprehensive look before she hesitantly turned and left the gym, glancing back several times in worry. He waited until the door was shut behind the last recruit.

Every time I turn around, Connor is trying to fight you. What happened?

He stood with his hands on his side, waiting for an explanation.

Same thing as the last time you called him off. He approached me and my partner and wouldn't take no for an answer. I'm sorry for hitting a guard but he wasn't easing up.

And you're not tempting him in any way?

I looked at him incredulously and then pointedly down at the t-shirt and sweats that I chose that morning.

Excuse me? Do you think I want that douchebag hitting on me? Like I'm just some desperate girl trying my hardest to be a damsel in distress?

I reached to put a stray hair behind my ear. Immediately, Ben's eyes locked on my forearm. Looking down at my arm, I could see that the bruises were already setting in from blocking Connor's punches.

Darcy, are you okay?

His voice cracked for the first time since I'd known him. He always seemed so confident and strong. Stepping in my direction, he grabbed my arms and inspected the bruises. Any kind of pain that I felt was instantly replaced by the tingling that his skin left in its wake.

Ben's eyes softened as he met eye contact with me. His guard was down for only a second before his stoic demeanor returned. He released my arms and took a step away from me, putting his head down and sighing.

I'm sorry. I didn't mean to accuse you. I know what Connor is capable of. Let me assure you that it will not happen again. If you need to return to your flat and ice your bruises, you are excused from weapon training for today.

No. I'm fine, really. Anyways, I was looking forward to knife throwing today. I'll just imagine the target is Connor.

I saw a hint of a smile on his face before he nodded in dismissal of me. I grabbed my jacket from the edge of the mat and walked toward the door. When I reached the exit, I looked back toward Ben. Standing in the same place I left him, he lifted his head and met eye contact with me. But this time, I didn't rush out the door. I returned his gaze and nodded at him.

Oh, and thanks for stopping him like you did.

Anytime, Darcy.

As my third week in training drew to a close, my chest became tighter and tighter. Although Connor did not approach me during lessons anymore, it was apparent that he held a bitter grudge toward me. The same fear that Kate had during her last week of protection haunted my dreams every night.

I wouldn't luck out like Kate did. When Noah claimed her, she was off limits to all other guards. Every night since then, Noah had come to our flat to spend time with Kate. They would talk until the early morning hours before he kissed her goodnight at the door and left.

As they became more and more comfortable with one another, they became more and more adorable. I didn't even mind being a third wheel at dinner. Seeing them so in love in a place like this made me so incredibly happy for them.

On the last day of my third week, my stomach was in knots. I couldn't bring myself to eat breakfast. Connor seemed to be even more cocky today than any day before, if that was possible. He constantly made eye contact with me, looked me from head to toe, and mumbled obscenities beneath his breath.

A couple times, I caught Ben watching Connor. There was no way to read his expression since he had returned to his unbreakable stoic demeanor. Although Kate attempted to comfort me with pats on the back, I couldn't help but worry that midnight would bring Connor straight to my door. The worst part was that there was nothing I could do about it.

The day went by in a blur as worry consumed my every thought. I seemed to be seeing Connor everywhere whether it was in the hall or walking past the classroom door during a lesson. Not a morsel of food had passed my lips that day. In fact, any thought of consuming a meal left my stomach churning worse than before.

Over dinner, Kate was unusually quiet as she picked at the food on her plate. I excused myself from the counter, having not touched a single item on my plate. Even thinking about Connor all day had left me feeling disgusting.

Getting in the shower, I scrubbed my skin raw as if I could cleanse myself of Connor. I stood letting the hot water sting my back. I stayed under the water until the steam in the shower became too much to breath in. Wrapping myself in a towel, I twisted my hair into a single French braid down my back.

The cool air in the hallway was a relief tonight after standing under the stinging hot water for so long. Getting dressed, I hopped under the covers and prayed for morning to come without any visitors. I continued to slip in and out of sleep for the next few hours.

Suddenly, a knock at the door echoed down the hallway to my room. I shot straight up out of bed and looked at the clock: a couple minutes past midnight. My fear had become my reality. Flinging my door open, I looked out in the hallway to find Kate looking out from her bedroom.

Fear filled her eyes as I hesitantly walked out of my room toward the kitchen. Another knock rang through the flat. I looked through the hole in the door. Panic set over me as Connor's face appeared on the other side of the door.

I could see him leaning in toward the door with his arms hanging above his head on the doorframe.

Kate, what do I do? It's Connor.

My whisper hissed desperately through the quiet apartment. She stood, interchanging her weight-bearing leg rapidly as if she had to pee.

I don't know, Darcy, there's nothing we can do. Even if we report him, they'll just ignore it because it boosts morale. They'll sweep it under the rug.

I can't do this. I can't.

Another knock. This time, Connor was getting impatient. There was nothing I could do. The longer I waited to open the door, the angrier he was getting and the worse off I was. I reached for the door handle and opened the door slowly. Connor's big smirky face was closer than expected.

Hey there, champ. I've been waiting for this night since the first time I laid eyes on you.

In that moment, I could have thrown up. My stomach churned in agony and my heart beat hard in my throat. He began advancing toward me through the doorway but was suddenly pulled backwards. Connor's expression was filled with surprise and anger.

To my astonishment, Ben stepped into view, still holding onto the back of Connor's shirt. He released his hold as soon as Connor attempted to wriggle free. Fixing his shirt from the manhandling he had just received, it was obvious that Connor was beyond annoyed at the disruption.

What are you doing here, Ben? This doesn't concern you. A claim is a claim.

I don't believe there's been a claim yet. Has there, Darcy?

Although the thought of getting claimed at all scared me to death, Connor would be the last person that I would want to claim me. Ben looked down at me, his eyes soft and reassuring yet guarded as Connor eyed the both of us. A small sense of relief washed over me and pulled me along in support of Ben.

No, there hasn't.

A growl came from Connor as he stepped back toward the door. Yet, Ben was quicker. He was in between Connor and I in a split second, blocking my vision of the hallway. Through gritted teeth, Connor stood his ground.

I was here first, Lewis. Step away. You know the rules.

I don't think I will, Connor. A claim has not yet been made. As your leader, I think you should be heading back to your dorm.

Ben's tone of voice did not merely give a suggestion but a command. The two stood face to face before Connor stepped down in obvious frustration.

This isn't over, Lewis.

She's mine now, Connor. You know the rules.

Connor's own words were thrown back in his face as Ben turned toward me and stepped through the doorway. He turned back toward Connor and shut the door in his face.

In the dark of the flat, I could see Ben's back rise along with his breathing. Kate had since retreated to her doorway where her head poked from behind the wooden frame. With his hands on the door, there was a long silence as he hung his head. Suddenly, Ben looked down the hall toward Kate, aware that we were not alone. The silhouette of her head disappeared, the sound of her door immediately following.

He turned around to face me, looking down to meet my eyes. Yet, they held no sign of romance or sexuality in them, only the same stony expression. How he was so successful in hiding his feelings in every situation, I had no idea. It was like he could shut himself off from the world surrounding him and simply function.

Where is your bedroom?

His eyes were intense as they looked down at me, waiting for my answer. I felt like a fool, standing in awkward silence as the words in my mind failed to be spoken. In disbelief, I walked off toward my room, the sound of his footsteps following behind me.

Once in my room, I heard the sound of my door shut behind us. I had reached the middle of the room before I turned around to see him lingering in the doorway. The light of the moon came through my window, illuminating the wooden floor and the white comforter on my bed.

Had it been a different situation entirely, the room might have been considered romantic. But it wasn't. No matter if he had saved me from Connor, I was still only a piece of property to a guard that had claimed me. Anger flooded into my chest and propelled the words that had gotten caught in my throat out at Ben.

So, what now? You've claimed me. What is your command, sir? Shall I dance for you like a puppet or just get in the bed and shut my mouth?

The wall that seemed to permanently obstruct his expressions fell momentarily. He seemed totally shocked by my outburst, his cheeks pink in embarrassment. But my anger only swelled to new heights.

I don't know why you looked so shocked. Isn't that what you're here for, what every guard is here for as soon as the three weeks are up?

He stepped away from the doorway, leading me to believe that he was going to approach me. Instead, he put his back against the wall and slid down to the ground. His hands went to his face, wearily rubbing its surface. The dark jeans that he wore were tight against his thighs with his knees bent in the air. Muscles protruded from his arms as he bent them toward his face. He wore a charcoal gray t-shirt and tennis shoes to match.

Seeing him in anything other than workout clothes both felt strange and thrilling. His hair was ruffled as if he had been running his hands through it in frustration. Even disheveled, I was unable to take my eyes off him. It was at this point that he dropped his hands and looked at me.

Just go to bed, Darcy. I am not here for anything.

The shock must have been apparent on my face as a corner of his mouth pulled up in amusement. He straightened his legs and placed his hands in his lap.

So, what's the point of you being here? You're just going to sit there and watch me sleep?

A deep chuckle escaped his chest and his eyes twinkled in entertainment.

It's all I've been waiting to do for the past three weeks.

The sarcasm dripped from his statement as he grinned from the floor up at me. His gaze dropped from my face to my pajamas quickly before he looked back down to his hands. I looked down at my outfit, realizing that I was underdressed for any company. In overwhelming worry after my shower, I had thoughtlessly grabbed a camisole and pair of cotton boxer shorts to wear. I was immediately aware that it was the least amount of clothes I had worn in front of him.

Blood rushed to my cheeks as I retreated to the cover of my bed comforter. Ben kept his head down until I was settled under the covers. His eyes were soft as he looked across the room at me.

Try to get some sleep, Darcy. Don't worry. I'm not moving from this spot.

I studied his expression before lying my head on my pillow. Carefully, I positioned myself where I could see him easily from across the room. Under his ruffled hair, his eyes were illuminated by the moonlight.

I don't know if it was utter exhaustion, the relief that Connor would not be accompanying me tonight, or the fact that I actually trusted Ben's statement that allowed my eyes to close. Sleep came quicker than I anticipated but nevertheless brought the same dreams that interrupted my sleep every night.

Suddenly, I was transported to the weapons room. It was dark except for a single spot in the middle of the floor. Fear filled my chest as I approached the spotlight, unable to stop my feet from moving me forward.

Then, I was not alone in the light. Margot Clarke stepped into the light with the same gray pant suit and sharp eyes cutting into my soul. A flash of light gleamed off the knife in her hand. To my surprise, I stood at attention as a soldier would to his commanding officer. As she arrived at my side, she took my hand and pressed the handle of the knife firmly in my palm.

Another circle of light illuminated the room. In it was a man tied to a chair, his head bowed down to hide his identity. Margot gestured for me to go to him, releasing her hold of the knife. My feet took me closer and closer to the man as if I was no longer in control of my own actions. As I grew closer and closer to him, he looked all too familiar.

Grabbing the hair on the back of his scalp, I pulled his drooping head up in order to see his face. My knife was at his neck as the same green eyes that haunted all my dreams looked at me, fear filling them. All at once, I could feel Margot behind me, the pressure of her command all too overwhelming.

Cut his throat, Darcy. It is for the good of the Society.

I fought the control that she had on me. I didn't want to be her puppet. More than that, I didn't want to kill Ben. The knife pressed deeper and deeper until a drop of blood ran down his neck. Desperately, I fought for control of my hands. His fear-filled eyes pierced into my soul until I let out a blood-curdling scream, breaking through the force that controlled my every move.

All at once, I felt hands on my arms. However, I was no longer dreaming. The scream that escaped my lungs was no dream and neither were the hands that gently grasped my arms. Opening my eyes, I saw the same green eyes filled with fear looking back at me. Ben was sitting next to me on the side of the bed, pulling me up from the pillow.

Darcy, Darcy. Are you okay?

I sat up and looked around the room. We were in my bedroom, not the weapons room. Margot was nowhere to be seen. I looked down at my hands, failing to find a knife as well as detecting complete control of my own movements. My gaze returned to his face as my breathing slowed.

Darcy, you were screaming your head off. What's wrong? Are you hurt?

Throat dry from the screaming, I managed to croak out a reply.

I'm fine.

Ben seemed confused by my nonchalant reply.

Do you do this every night?

Almost.

His hands were still around my arms as I sat there. The breath that I managed to catch was taken away by his closeness. The warmth of his body emanated from him like a heater, the smell of him filling my lungs. It was obvious that he had showered before he came, the scent of soap still clung to his skin and soft tendrils of his hair curled at the ends. A rapid knock sounded at the door with the sound of Kate on the other side.

Darcy, are you alright?

I met Ben's eyes as we both realized that she thought it was him who made me scream. Still looking into his eyes, I reassured Kate of my safety.

Yeah, just a bad dream.

Ok... well let me know if you need anything.

Her footsteps receded from the other side of the door as she returned to her own room. Ben had not broken eye contact, still studying my face for any sign that I lied to Kate about being okay.

She thought you screamed because of me.

I nodded and looked down at my arms. His arms cupped my elbows, my hands sitting in my lap. Ben's hands were large and warm. Shocked by my desire for him to stay, I raised my head once again to meet his eye contact. His expression was soft, without a guard to hide his true feelings. I could feel the pull between us, like a magnet naturally drawing us closer to one another.

At the same time, he seemed to notice our closeness and released his hold. Standing up quickly, he crossed the room and returned to his place on the floor. Once again, his face was stoic and his posture taut.

I wanted him close again, but it was obvious he felt the exact opposite. My mind searched for a reason why he came here tonight. To get back at Connor for his countless acts of rebellion toward Ben's leadership?

He sat with his head against the wall and eyes closed, evidently finished talking to me. A slight twinge of rejection came over me. Laying back down, I turned my back toward him and pulled the covers to my neck.

It was the sound of his breath, the rhythm of it that lulled me back to sleep. Regardless of his intentions, Ben saved me from Connor once again. Romance was the last thing on anyone's mind here in the Society. Yet, no matter how often I told myself this, my heart and my mind wouldn't agree.

VII.

CHARADES

The sound of my alarm woke me up from a dead sleep. It seemed that the little sleep I had without restless dreams was interrupted by my alarm clock. I turned over to hit the top of the clock and opened my eyes. Reality of the night before dawned on me, sitting up and looking toward the door. Ben was gone.

Throwing on jogging capris and a white racerback tank top, I kept my hair woven in one long braid down my back and threw on tennis shoes. Opening my bedroom door, I made my way to the bathroom only to be grabbed by Kate upon my arrival.

Darcy, what the heck happened last night? Ben talked down Connor?!? I had no idea he was even interested in claiming you. He's always so serious and has never claimed a recruit before! I didn't even think he liked that rule…

I smiled down at her as she took a breath from her long strand of words. She looked at me expectantly with her hands on my arms.

When I heard you scream last night, I was so scared. I thought he had hurt you. Not a lot of guards come for gentle romance, you know. I can't believe Ben claimed you! Darcy, why aren't you saying anything?

I laughed and looked down at her in amusement.

Because you've barely taken a breath.

Well? What happened?

I don't know. Connor came to the door and was about to walk in when Ben stepped in between us. I'm kind of worried for today's classes if Connor is still as mad as he was last night.

Connor doesn't need an excuse to be aggressive. He's always looking for a good fight. But I heard you scream...

Just had another one of my wonderful dreams.

She and I had talked about my trouble sleeping before. However, this time, I wasn't alone in my bedroom. Kate didn't seem to believe me as I reassured her of my safety. As I made my way for my toothbrush, she gave me a look of doubt out of the corner of her eyes.

Well, if he hurt you, I'll string him up by his toes and beat him.

A burst of laughter came from my mouth as I imagined tiny Kate stringing up the over six foot in height Ben by his toes. At the same time, being her partner in training for over three weeks made me wonder if it was possible. She could definitely hold her own in a fight.

So, how's things going with Noah?

Oh, so you want me to spill the dirt on Noah, but you can't describe your night with Ben?

Nothing happened, I swear.

You mean to tell me that a guy that hot was in your bedroom all night and nothing happened? Please.

Kate! I swear! I wouldn't lie to you. I have no idea why he even came. He just sat there by my door on the ground.

He just sat there?

I nodded my head as I brushed my teeth. Kate looked as confused as I felt. Spitting into the sink, Kate leaned against the counter waiting for the next piece of information.

It's not like I wanted to be claimed... I just don't understand why he came. Isn't the whole point of the guards claiming a recruit... well, for sex?

I thought so but Noah hasn't made a move yet. He's being so respectful. We just talk all night and then kiss at the door. It seems that we are both exceptions to the rule.

Yeah, but at least everyone saw you and Noah coming.

She seemed shocked by my statement, blood rushing to her cheeks yet again.

What? Everyone did not see me and Noah getting together!

Oh, totally. You guys were all smiles around each other. You couldn't even sit still as he taught business class!

We both burst into laughter as we made our way into the kitchen for breakfast. After our awkward conversation in the bathroom, we kept the conversation casual, talking about upcoming exams and lessons.

Down in the gym, we stretched and prepared for that day's lesson. My heart beat fast as Ben walked in the door. His hair had been brushed since I last saw him and he had changed into athletic shorts and a t-shirt. Rings under his eyes showed his lack of sleep from the night before.

I watched him walk across the gym toward the rest of the recruits, looking for any sign of him remembering last night. He scanned the room before finding me next to Kate on the gym mat in our small circles of friends.

As he approached our group, he cleared his throat and made direct eye contact with me.

Darcy, can I speak to you for a moment?

The recruits in my circle looked up in surprise. There was never a one-on-one chat between Ben and recruits outside of the lesson time. I could tell by their faces that they were curious about the reason for the meeting.

I stood up and followed Ben to an area near the wall past the gym mats. He stopped and turned toward me, the rings under his eyes darker than when I saw him from a distance.

Did you sleep at all last night?

No. Darcy, we need to talk. Connor is going to be here any moment. If he thinks at all that my claim wasn't real, he'll show right back up at your doorstep tonight. That's why I think we should let everyone think that it's real.

Though his words seemed logical, I couldn't help but be disappointed by the way he easily admitted there was nothing between us. He pushed his hair back from his forehead. It had grown in the past few weeks, allowing small waves to form around his face.

I thought a claim was a claim?

Connor doesn't necessarily abide by the rules. Even rules as vulgar as he is. Just trust me. We have to make this seem real.

And how do you propose we do that?

Well, guards who claim recruits usually have conversations outside of lessons. We should make an attempt to have casual conversations before and after class.

Okay, easy enough.

Since a claim holds a physical meaning to it, we should act like people who have… intimate relations… which means small touches, standing or sitting close…

Yeah, I get it. So, this has to be around everyone or just Connor?

Everyone. You never know who talks to who. Word could travel back to him. And if it does, you'll be sorry when he shows up at your door. Connor is a dirtbag. Believe me, he shares stories.

A chill went down my back as even the slightest idea of what he could be sharing with his peers went through my mind. It seemed I had no choice but to pretend to be involved with Ben.

Okay, if it means keeping him away.

Alright, well here he comes now.

Connor had already crossed the expanse of the gym, heading toward where Ben and I stood.

Well, aren't you just a cute couple? Ben, you look tired. I assume you both got little sleep last night.

That doesn't concern you, Connor.

Oh, I'm sure Ben will fill me in later when you're not around.

The look that Ben gave Connor told the exact opposite. I felt Ben's hand around my waist as he gently guided me away from Connor and back toward the recruits. I could feel Connor's glare on my back as we escaped his questioning.

Alright, recruits, time for today's lessons. Start with your run. Twenty laps today.

There was a moment of hesitation as the recruits watched Ben release his hold on me, directing me back to Kate's side. Kate even had a look of disbelief on her face, matching every recruit in the room.

You want to make that thirty? I suggest you start running.

Ben seemed to be in no mood for any kind of resistance today. Connor joined his side at the front of the class as the recruits jumped up and began their run, avoiding the increased number of laps. I ran between Kate and Hannah for the duration of the run.

Ben made an attempt to look at me each time that I passed, Connor witnessing his attention to me. As he watched his superior, he seemed suspicious. I had a feeling it was going to take a long time for Connor to give up on his pursuit of me. And Ben's involvement only made him want it more.

That night, I was in the bathroom brushing my teeth before I went to bed when I heard a knock at the door. Fear and visions of Connor returning to my doorstep froze me in place. I quickly spit out the toothpaste in my mouth and made my way to the hallway.

Kate and Noah came out from her bedroom as I exited the bathroom. Kate met eye contact with me and blushed, smiling at me as I raised my eyebrows. She pushed his arm toward the door. He looked down at her and then at me, seeming to understand both of our fears. Making his way to the door, he opened it and looked pleased.

Hey, man, how's it going?

I'm good.

Ben stepped through the door and finished talking with Noah before looking down the hall toward me. He wore jeans again with a sweatshirt to replace his previous t-shirt. His hair was still damp from his shower. Kate cleared her throat and Noah followed her playfully back into her room, leaving Ben and I looking at each other.

I didn't know you were coming back.

Well, we can't chance Connor coming back, can we? He lives down the hall from me. If he notices that I never come to your room, he definitely won't believe our act.

Yeah, I guess. You can sleep on the couch if you want.

No, Noah is my best friend here at the facility and Kate is yours but... I was raised to trust no one. It's best for it to stay between the two of us.

Okay, whatever you say. I just have to finish getting ready for bed. I'll be there in a second.

He nodded and disappeared into my bedroom. I couldn't help but appreciate how he even made a sweatshirt look charming. Returning to the bathroom, I looked in the mirror. My hair was in a messy bun and my eyeliner was smeared from not being totally washed off in the shower.

I let my hair down from the bun and used tissue paper to clean off the remnants of my makeup. The t-shirt and shorts that I wore fit loosely on my figure. Realizing that it was ridiculous to try looking cute for bed, I rolled my eyes and left the bathroom.

Going to the kitchen for a glass of water, I could smell the scent of Ben's soap, clean and masculine, as I passed my room. There was no sign of him from the doorway. The cabinet door swung open, revealing a shelf full of glasses. When I closed it, Ben was on the other side of the door. Nearly jumping out of my skin, I clutched my chest in surprise and glared at him, grinning down at me.

You should really pay more attention in class. You would have heard me and had a better reaction than jumping a foot in the air.

I didn't realize that we were in class. Sorry, professor.

He ran his hands through his hair and leaned on the counter. His jeans fit him nicely, not too loose or tight. With his arms crossed against his chest, he watched as I filled my glass with water from the tap.

You need a drink? There are glasses in the cabinet behind you.

He shrugged in refusal and looked around the large room toward the living area.

They set you recruits up nicely. My place is half the size but, of course, we don't share with one another.

Have you never been in a recruit's flat before me?

Shaking his head, he looked down at his shoes then back at me.

No. Never had a reason to.

Oh, and what about the guards' rule about claiming recruits?

He laughed and shook his head in disbelief.

I don't participate or approve. Do you think I just go around claiming women all the time?

His eyes were intense as he studied me, waiting for my reply. I shrugged, not knowing what to say. However, I couldn't help but feel a sense of relief at his confession. Drinking the rest of the water, I put the cup in the sink and walked off toward my room.

I hadn't realized how chilled I got until the warmth of the blankets hit my legs. The sound of the door clicking shut was followed by a small thud. Ben was back in his spot on the ground, with his head down on his crossed arms.

Then why now?

Ben raised his head and looked at me. He took a moment to remember our conversation from the kitchen and understand to what my question pertained. The silence that followed my question was heavy.

I don't know.

His tone of voice did not give the impression of avoidance or flippant decision-making, but as if he truly did not know why he was there, as if he had asked himself that same question.

A week went by the same way: Ben would come to my room at night, make conversation with me throughout the day, walk me to an occasional class, and make physical contact with me every once in a while. A small touch on the back or arm.

Connor seemed to only get more and more suspicious of us as the week went by. His paranoia only grew the more fatigued

Ben looked. His exhaustion had gotten so bad that he yawned through classes and was defeated at every practice fight.

As he talked with me outside one of my afternoon classes, he leaned against the wall beside me and closed his eyes. I looked up at him. The rings under his eyes were even darker and his face was pale.

Ben, you need some sleep. Go back to your room and take a nap.

I can't. I have a meeting today with the Board. A report of how the recruits are doing. Connor's coming this way.

Connor approached us with the same arrogance that came natural to his every move. His smirk sent chills down my back even with the warmth of Ben hovering next to me.

How cute are the new love birds? Ben, you really must take a break every once in a while. You look exhausted. Love does not suit you well. That fight this morning was just too easy.

Buzz off, Connor.

Ben pushed his hair out of his face and looked down at me, ignoring the harassment from his peer. The sound of Ben's beeper went off and reminded him of his meeting. He made meaningful eye contact that only I saw before he pushed off the wall.

I'll see you tonight, okay?

Okay.

Ben brushed his hand against my cheek before walking off in the direction of the executive hall. Connor only seemed entertained by our show of affection. He placed his hand on the wall above me and looked down at me, uncomfortably close.

Just let me know if he's not able to satisfy you, sweetheart. I'll be there in a moment's notice.

I don't think that will ever happen, Connor.

Your loss, champ.

I had heard enough, pushing past him and knocking his hand off the wall. As I walked into my classroom, I heard him mumble something under his breath before the door closed behind me.

Luckily, my now soured attitude was improved as I found a seat next to Kate. She saw my disgusted expression as I sat down at the desk and placed my textbooks in front of me.

Connor?

I nodded and told her about his offer. She made a gagging noise and rubbed my back in consolation.

Ugh, he's disgusting. But now you're with me… and… Noah is teaching the class, so your day just got like a hundred times better.

I couldn't help but smile at her positivity, her sweet brown eyes sparkling with excitement. Luckily, with Noah teaching the lesson, the topic was easier to digest than if Mr. Monotonous down the hall were teaching it.

The content covered the upheaval of various governments throughout history from the Nazis to modern-day revolutions across the world. I couldn't help but wonder how many of these coup d'états were a natural occurrence or an event incubated by the Society.

When the foundations that manage the actions of a large group of people are destroyed, societies collapse.

Noah's words stuck in my head the rest of the day. I had allowed myself to get lost in the luxury of the Society, the lessons forced down our throats, and the drama that came with the recruits and guards. I had forgotten how I got here, how everyone got here.

Later that night, Ben knocked on the door at the usual time. Noah's words still filled my head as I opened the door for Ben. Still pale, he walked straight into my room and sat down on the ground.

How was your meeting today?

Same as always. They listen and ask questions, taking notes the entire time. Their discussion doesn't start until I leave.

Was Margot Clarke there to make you feel tiny?

She is the President so, yes, she was there.

His tone was snarky as he looked across the room. As soon as it left his mouth, I saw regret fill his eyes.

I'm sorry.

His face looked even more pale in the light from the lamp. It seemed as though he could pass out at any moment.

You need sleep, Ben. You're going to make yourself sick. Go sleep on the couch.

I already told you no.

Then lay here with me.

His immediate expression of shock most likely matched mine as the words slipped out of my mouth. The guard he usually utilized was down, exhaustion probably making it impossible to maintain this late in the day.

What?

I'm not coming onto you. You need sleep and this bed is huge. Just come lay on the other side and sleep.

No, I'll be fine. I don't want to make you feel uncomfortable.

Well, it was my idea so that excuse isn't valid. Connor is starting to doubt this whole thing. You look like you're dying and I'm fine. He even offered to come over if you weren't satisfying me enough.

Even without Connor there, the disgust of his offer was too much. My stomach churned at the thought of it. Ben's eyes went from heavy with exhaustion to intense with anger.

He offered to come over if I'm not enough for you? This isn't working. He doesn't believe any of this. I'm killing myself for nothing. He's never going to stop.

Ben had gotten up from his place on the ground and began pacing the length of my closet. Running his hands over his face and through his hair, he looked like he was about to explode.

I got up and walked over to him, stepping in front of his obsessive path. He was forced to stop his pacing as he came face to face with me. Looking down, I could see that he felt helpless.

Ben, it's not even been a week since we've been doing this. You're exhausted and it's making you panic. It will work but only if you get some sleep. Come on.

Though he still seemed unsure, he let me guide him over to the opposite side of the bed. My hands pressed against his firm back, immediately feeling heated from the contact. I left him there to get under the covers however he preferred and walked over to my side.

He watched as I crawled under the covers before kicking off his shoes and climbing in. There was quite a bit of distance between the two of us, but I could still feel his warmth under the covers.

Sleep was immediate for Ben, his breathing slowed and his body stilled as soon as he laid down. Having spent every night for the past week sitting on the ground, he must have been utterly exhausted. He was lucky he hadn't become ill from the lack of sleep.

I lay there awake for some time, very aware of Ben's presence next to me. He had been careful to leave plenty of space between us, laying practically on the edge of the bed. Finally, my eyes became heavy as I listened to the rise and fall of his breath, the rhythm soothing in a way.

The sound of the alarm was the first thing that woke me up in the morning. I sat up shocked that morning had already come. It was the first night in a long time that I hadn't tossed and turned with nightmares. I felt more rested than I had since before my mother passed away.

I looked beside me to find Ben still sleeping. He had slept past the alarm and remained laying with his arms above his head in a deep sleep. Reaching to prod the arm closest to me, I almost felt guilty for waking him. His eyes blinked opened and looked at me.

Sorry to wake you but you still have to get ready for class and you don't have any clothes here.

Ben sat up, his hair disheveled and shirt riding up his back. I could see the dip of his dimples on his lower back, his skin smooth. He bent over the side of the bed to put his shoes back on before standing up and turning toward me.

Thanks, I probably would have overslept. I better get going.

Okay, let me walk you out.

I followed him as he walked into the hallway and toward the door. To both of our surprise, Noah and Kate sat at the counter eating breakfast, smiling over their pancakes at one another. Kate looked shocked as she saw the rumpled Ben walking out from the hallway.

Ben seemed to be thrown off guard as two sets of eyes stared back at him over the counter. After a moment's hesitation, he nodded his head in greeting and walked out the door. I looked back at the two love birds eating their breakfast. Kate proceeded to put a bite of pancake in her mouth, smiling slightly at me as she chewed. Noah was the first to speak.

Morning, Darcy. Of all the years I've known Ben, I don't think I've ever seen him like that. But, of course, it's not like we've had any slumber parties.

I took you as a slumber party kind of guy, Noah.

He met my eye contact over his pancakes as I laughed and ran back toward my room to get ready for the day. I couldn't help but think of how much better Ben looked after getting a night's sleep. The color had come back to his face and the rings under his eyes were barely existent.

No longer worried for his health, I was more worried of what he thought of me after I forced him into my bed. Though he seemed grateful for the sleep, I just hoped I hadn't crossed a line or depicted myself as a girl used to having men in her bed.

Hopefully with some sleep, Ben had changed his mind about our charade being useless. If I had to admit it, there were times that I forgot it was all pretend.

VIII.

SHEEP'S CLOTHING

When the foundations that manage the actions of a large group of people are destroyed, societies collapse.

No matter how hard I tried, Noah's statement ran through my head constantly. After getting dressed, I headed back toward the kitchen, stomach rumbling with the smell of pancakes in the air. Noah was placing his dishes in the sink as I walked into the kitchen.

Darcy, sorry to miss you but I've got to go prepare for class. Hope you like my pancakes. It was my grandmother's recipe. With Kate's help, the pancakes turned out round this time.

What were they before?

Don't ask.

We all laughed before Noah kissed Kate goodbye and walked out the door. Kate sat sipping her orange juice beside a plate of half-used syrup.

I grabbed a plate from the cabinet and claimed two small pancakes for myself, smearing butter and drizzling syrup across the top of them. Sitting next to Kate, I placed the first bite of pancake in my mouth.

Oh my gosh, these are delicious.

Kate smiled over her the rim of her glass before setting it down on the counter in front of her.

Ben seemed surprised getting caught leaving for once. He's usually gone before I wake up.

Yeah, he slept in today by accident.

She nodded her head and studied me as I ate my pancakes. I kept hearing Ben's voice claiming he didn't trust anyone with the truth about us. Though she seemed like she was waiting for more information, I quickly changed the subject.

The first day we met, you were pretty outspoken about the Society. Aren't you happy here?

I'm happier now that I have Noah, but I still don't trust this place. There are rumors about what they do, you know.

What kind of rumors?

You know Brendan? He's already been told that when he finishes his training, he's going to stay at the facility. Since he's so good with computers, he's been training to become their IT guy here. Guess there's been problems with their system.

Oh, I didn't know that he did that.

Anyways, they let him fix their network which has all the information about the Society. Most of it is locked so he can't read it but there's low level cases that he can see without it sending a red flag to the Society.

Kate had grown very serious. Her voice was low as she leaned forward, as if someone could be listening on the other side of the door.

He said they aren't just ending wars, feeding the hungry, and curing diseases like they claim they are. He found the beginning of research done on biological weapons. We're talking about chemicals that could kill a large number of people when released. Now what kind of benevolent society would be researching that type of thing?

What else does he have access to?

Don't know. We got interrupted when a guard passed us in the hall. All I know is that he's got access to a lot... and it's not all roses like they make it seem. Why do you ask?

I don't know. I just can't shake this feeling that something is not right about this place. Maybe we should ask Brendan more questions today.

Darcy, you better be careful. I wouldn't go around stepping on a giant's toes. You might regret it.

Her warning stayed with me as we made our way to that morning's lessons. As we walked into the gym, I spotted Brendan sitting on the mat closest to the wall. He sat alone, many of the recruits not having yet arrived. I took this opportunity to try to get some information out of him.

As I approached him, he waved his hand in greeting to both Kate and me. She gave me a look of warning before we reached where Brendan sat.

Hey, Brendan. How's it going?

Pretty good, you?

I'm fine. So, Kate and I were talking this morning about what you do here. She was telling me some of the rumors she's heard about what the Society actually does.

Kate, I told you that in confidence.

No, no. She wasn't telling anyone but me and she was very careful about it.

Kate gave me a look of gratefulness before turning her attention back to Brendan.

You can trust me. So why does the Society let you maintain their computer systems as a recruit?

They have only been training me to become part of their IT team. I don't have full access yet until I've completed my training. The only reason I have access to what I do is because their system has been glitchy lately.

What else have you seen besides the biological weapons?

Brendan looked around the gym before leaning in toward me and Kate.

They have detailed record of every recruit and member of the Society. Their system maintains their finances, communication with field members, and information on projects they are working on. This system is absolutely essential to the success of the Society.

So, what if the system were to go down?

The system doesn't go down. They've designed it to have backup servers and countless firewalls. It's not something they just threw together on a whim.

How many members are there?

I have no idea, but I would guess hundreds, maybe even thousands.

Brendan glanced around the gym for any new recruits that may have arrived.

Darcy, there is more to this Society than they're letting on. It's not something you should mess with. It's bigger than any of us could have imagined.

With the second warning of the morning, I chose to end the topic as other recruits began to file in for the morning session. I couldn't help but wonder what it was the Society was hiding and how exactly they intended to use the recruits to accomplish it.

Kate leaned over and nudged my arm.

Rumor has it that after all the recruits pass their exams this week, specialized training is going to be assigned to every recruit based on their field assignment. They want us prepared whenever it's time for deployment.

When you say rumor has it, do you mean Noah enjoys some nice pillow talk?

96

Kate's face blushed and she bent her head down lower toward mine.

Shhh! If any word gets out that Noah gives me heads up, he'd get in so much trouble.

Okay, okay. I promise I won't tell but only if you give me heads up, too.

I smiled in reassurance to her before she laughed at my poor attempt at blackmail. Looking up, I realized that all the other recruits had already arrived in addition to Noah and Ben, who stood in front of the recruits. Kate seemed to also realize this as she perked up at the sight of him.

Alright, recruits. Today, we will be evaluating you on the basics that you have been learning for the last month or so. The exams will test fitness, stealth, self-defense, and handling of the bow staff. If you pass these, the next and more intense phase of training begins.

Ben was no longer disheveled as he stood before the recruits. His hair had been tamed since I last saw him and he had changed into a fresh pair of shorts and t-shirt.

I found it odd that he hadn't made any attempt to talk with me before class started. Maybe Connor's absence had something to do with it. Yet, I couldn't help but wonder if I had pushed him too far the night before. It was obvious that he was avoiding making eye contact with me.

Noah and Ben both took turns testing the recruits and documenting the results. Exams ranged from a timed run and duels between recruits to obstacle courses requiring silent completion. Noah studied the recruits as partners sparred with bow staffs.

By the end of the four-hour block of exams, every recruit was sweating and gulping down their water. Relief spread across the gym as Ben dismissed the recruits to their break before afternoon classes began. Kate sprinted over to Noah who caught her out of the air. They embraced before walking out of the gym, smiling and whispering to one another.

I lingered behind, both trying to avoid being an awkward third wheel and steal a moment with Ben before I went back to the flat. He sat on the edge of the boxing ring, making notes on his writing pad. It was obvious that he hadn't realized that we were the only two left in the room.

As I approached him, he stood up and closed his notebook. He sat it down on the boxing ring behind him and put his hands in his pockets casually. His cool demeanor had me doubting any conversation I had already thought of in my head.

Hey, I missed you before class.

Yeah, you seemed busy talking to other recruits, so I figured I'd leave you alone.

Oh. I didn't see you come in.

An awkward silence filled the space between us as we both stood unsure of how one another felt. Why was I so afraid of how he felt about me? This was all an act anyway. He was just putting Connor in his place this entire time. I was about to break the silence when Ben erupted with words.

Look, I'm sorry for last night. I shouldn't have even got in your bed. I know it was your idea, but I should've said no. That was unprofessional.

I couldn't help but let out a laugh. He seemed almost hurt by my outburst and met eye contact with me, his green eyes vulnerable.

Ben, none of this is professional. It was my idea and if I was insulted by it, I wouldn't have offered. You needed the sleep. I was worried I crossed a line with you.

No… you didn't.

Rather than relief spreading across his face as expected, his eyes showed torment as if he were fighting himself internally. He looked away as the gym door slammed shut. His guard went up immediately as he stood at attention at the approaching individual.

Looking across the gym, I watched as the President of the Society walked across the hard gym floor to where we stood at the boxing ring. Ben was stiff as a board as the President shook his hand.

Benjamin. I assume your report of the test results are ready?

Yes, ma'am. Here you are.

Margot accepted his notebook and placed it under her arm for safekeeping. It was then that she turned her attention to me.

Darcy Bishop, it seems that you are getting along well here at the facility. I am very pleased with your test scores.

Thank you.

If you don't mind, I would like a word alone with Benjamin.

Her words were curt, her dismissive body language giving me no other option but to leave the gym. As I crossed the expanse to the door, I chanced taking a look back.

Margot stood with her back to me, but it was clear she was not too pleased with Ben. He stood at attention, extremely taut and stoic as she spoke rather closely to his face. Before either one noticed, I slipped out the door and went back to the flat for lunch and a shower before afternoon exams.

I couldn't understand how anyone could follow such a cold and severe woman like Margot. Her effect on Ben showed that one of the ways she controlled her subordinates was through fierce reprimanding.

That night when Ben arrived, his stoic demeanor had not worn off. He walked straight into the bedroom and sat down on the ground without saying a single word. As I followed him into the room, I looked down at him puzzled.

I take it the conversation with the President did not go well,
Benjamin.

My purposeful mocking of the President's formality
seemed to conjure no humor. He continued to sit there staring at
the wall parallel to him, void of expression. I retreated to the
warmth of my bed as I waited for a reply. When none came, I sat
there searching for any reason their conversation would have
affected me at all. Then it hit me.

She doesn't want you involved with me, does she?

Ben's eyes shot in my direction in an abrupt break of
character. He exhaled a long and heavy breath before speaking.

It's not just you, any recruit. She wants me focused on our
mission.

Oh, but the other guards can claim any piece of tail they
want?

There are higher expectations placed on me as head of the
guards.

So, if she doesn't want you involved with recruits, why are
you here?

He sat silent, staring off in the distance yet again. His use
of silence to get away with not answering questions was starting to
infuriate me.

Ben. I'm not falling for that silent treatment. And I'm not
believing you when you say you don't know. Frankly, if you can't
answer me, just go.

His head whipped in my direction at my frankness. My anger had managed to break through the guard he used so often, his eyes filled with hurt and confusion. He ran his hands through his hair, something I noticed he did when he was anxious.

I can't leave.

Well, then answer the question.

I don't want Connor to come back.

Are you always going to use him as an excuse?

Look at what he did to your arms.

I looked down at my bare arms, still dark in spots on my forearms from blocking Connor's punches. Ben's eyes were angry as he looked at the remnants of the deep bruises.

That was in a self-defense class. It's not like he would be throwing punches if he came over at night.

Any man who is willing to hit a woman is not particular about when and where he does it. He was willing to do it in front of a group of people. There's no telling what he would do to you in private.

Chills ran down my spine as the thought crossed my mind. It was clear Ben had no respect for his coworker. I could tell he was becoming heated, so I quickly redirected the conversation away from Connor's tendency for abuse.

Regardless, do you really think he conducts bed-checks every night?

Connor is persistent and a backstabber. I wouldn't put it past him. He would be here in an instant if he knew you and I weren't together.

Why do you even care? Why is it any of your business who claims me?

Because I don't want anyone else to have you.

Immediate regret filled his face as the heat of the moment forced the truth out of his mouth. I sat, mouth gaping in shock at his confession.

What?

You heard me. I can't stand by and watch you be claimed like property. They don't deserve you, especially Connor. That first night I came to your door, I couldn't get it out of my head that he would be there. I had showered and gone to bed... but I couldn't sleep. I just tossed and turned. I was miserable thinking about the things he's done to other recruits and I couldn't let that happen to you. So, I threw on clothes and came here. When I saw him in front of your door, I thought I was too late.

Ben dropped his eyes to where his hands laid in his lap. He almost seemed defeated, realizing that he could never get back the words he poured out to me. My chest fluttered as he sat there waiting for my reaction.

Darcy, please, just go to sleep. I've already made a fool of myself tonight. Just forget I said anything.

But I don't want to forget it.

He looked at me, eyes wide at first then soft. In the dim light, I could swear I saw a corner of his mouth pull upwards. Words eluded both of us as we sat in silence, looking across the room at one another.

Are you going to try to kill yourself again sitting on the floor all night or are you coming up here?

Ben seemed to weigh the consequences of his actions before slowly standing up and walking to the opposite side of the bed. Kicking his shoes off, he crawled under the covers and laid on his back. Carefully, I laid down on my side of the bed, making sure not to cross onto his half of the bed.

I turned the lamp on my bedside table off and pulled the covers to my neck. We both lay in the bed looking up at the ceiling, the glow of the moon outside illuminating the room.

Why do you scream in your sleep so much?

Nightmares. I've had them since my mom died.

Oh... what are they about?

Different things. Mostly about her.

He seemed to pause, absorbing the information. I had intentionally left out the nightmare about him.

What was she like?

She was the most beautiful person I've ever met: strong yet gentle, patient, loving, wise. Her hair and eyes were brown, both soft and flecked with gold. There was never a time in my life where I felt like our family was incomplete. She tried so hard to be

everything I needed, so hard on herself, so determined... She died
from breast cancer several months before I came here.

I'm sorry.

Thanks.

My parents passed away eight years ago. They were the
ones who created this Society. It was always their dream to make
the world a better place: cure diseases, prevent famine, end wars.
They were in South Sudan helping to rebuild a village that had
been burned down in a raid when another attack occurred.
Dozens of people died that night, villagers and volunteers.

Ben, I'm so sorry. I didn't know. I just figured you were
one of the guards whose family was involved in the Society.

I guess we have more in common than you thought.

His voice was uneven as we laid there sharing with each
other about our parents. I stretched my hand out toward the middle
of the bed, following the warmth of his arm. Finding his hand, I
wrapped my fingers around his. His hand was stiff at first but then
softened as he enveloped my hand in his.

We laid there; hands held between us as we fell asleep in
the moonlight. As I drifted to sleep, I couldn't help but notice a
similarity between Ben and the Influencers: they were not what
they appeared to be.

IX.

BLUEPRINTS

During the week following our exams, each recruit was assigned a specific topic of study which would pertain to their field assignment. While I was training in etiquette, hospitality, and various languages, Kate was placed in advanced chemistry and biology classes.

Brendan, of course, was assigned more computer courses as he continued his training for the Society's IT department. The red-haired Hannah was consumed in government courses. Other friends that I had made during training held varying topics: Sam, a short, chiseled blonde studied architecture and the tall, lanky African American, Dalia, the field of medicine.

The morning schedule did not change much with the new phase of training. The four-hour block of time was still reserved for physical training. However, the training had become more intense and complex.

We could no longer choose our partners for practice. Instead, partners were chosen at random and a bracket was created to determine the winner. The bottom half of the recruits would have to run an additional twenty laps after lessons were over. It was not uncommon for recruits to walk out of the gym each day either bruised or bleeding.

Afternoons still held general studies for the first class, yet, split off into specialized studies for the rest of the time. Since Kate and I had been assigned different areas, I did not see her as much during the afternoon. We made a point to eat lunch together every day to discuss our classes. Of course, the subject would always end up on Noah and how cute he was when he said this or did that.

I found their romance endearing but couldn't fight the feeling that it would all have to end when she was deployed to the field and Noah was left behind to train new recruits. Seeing how happy she was, I couldn't bring myself to ask her their plans for that point in the future. Yet, the more that I got to know Ben, the same fear hung over my head.

Walking down the hall after my class had ended, I glanced into a classroom in passing. Standing hunched over one of the lab tables was Sam, his blonde hair pushed back from his forehead in frustration. I backtracked a couple of steps before entering the room, first scanning for other inhabitants.

Hey, Sam. What's wrong?

He glanced up, not realizing he had company. His eyes immediately returned to the blueprints in front of him.

Oh, hey, Darcy. Nothing, I'm having a hard time learning some of the new curriculum they've introduced in my architecture class.

107

Well, I have no idea what I'm looking at but talk me through it.

As he spoke, he continued to furrow his brow over the blueprint in front of him. His hand traced lines up and down the paper as he explained his dilemma.

So, they've been covering how to build structures that properly bear the weight of the material. And this facility is built into a mountain, right?

Wait. The blueprint is of this facility? Let me see this.

I lurched toward the table and turned the paper slightly more toward me. Sam continued his study of the drawing beside me.

Yeah, I found it in the back of one of their cabinets.

There was no doubt that the blueprint was for the facility. Not many buildings are built into the middle of a mountain nor do they have two gyms, five stories of apartments, an executive suite, and its own medical unit.

I looked over the drawing and noticed there was a small area drawn beneath the main rooms that was labeled as the air, water, and waste filtration system. That would explain how we all survived here underground.

Yet, what I found intriguing was a line that diverged away from the facility altogether. I ran my finger along its path.

What is this?

That's how members of the Society get to and from the facility. It's how recruits are deployed into the field and how executives take their business trips.

How do you get there?

They've got it locked down. Only way in is to get past their security system.

And this is the IT department here?

A small square was just next to the tunnel entrance, connected through only one door. It seemed the largest and most weight bearing rooms were the weapons room and the gymnasium.

Yes. I didn't realize that you were so interested in architecture.

I'm not. Just this place.

He seemed to be puzzled by my statement but continued to talk me through what he didn't understand about the structure.

Being built into the middle of a mountain, this facility must have an immense amount of pressure weighing on it. Whoever built it must have been knowledgeable. If they had missed even one area needing more support, the whole thing would crumble.

Sam didn't know as he spoke in wonderment of their design that he was planting a seed in my mind. A seed that I couldn't help but water. I helped him as much as I could before I said my goodbye and left for dinner.

Kate was already in the flat making spaghetti when I walked through the door.

Did your class really go that long?

No, I talked to Sam on my way up. He needed help with his architecture class.

Oh, that was nice of you. Do you know much about architecture?

Enough.

I couldn't help but smile as the seed sprouted from the soil in my mind. The idea that had constantly lingered in my mind could no longer be contained.

Kate, I think I'm going to take down the Society.

She dropped the spoon of sauce in her hand, splattering the red liquid all over the counters and wall around the stove.

Darcy, that's not something you say lightly or something you do easily.

I know. But I think I could do it.... With a little help....

She caught the meaning behind my pauses as she continued to wipe the red splatter from the wall. Whirling around, she pointed her finger at me in warning.

Oh, no. I'm not getting involved in this. You want to die, be my guest. But there's no way that I'm joining that party.

Please, Kate! I can't do this without you. You know about the Society. You have connections with Noah and the other recruits---

Darcy, it's a death wish. There's no way we could do it.

Just think about it. I think I have a plan, but I can't do it alone.

Kate still seemed unsure about the entire idea.

Kate, if we don't do something, the Society is only going to keep hurting people. You saw what they were researching. Do you think they're intending on using those biological weapons for good?

She seemed to be drowning in inner turmoil as she deliberated her next choice. Finally, she shrugged her shoulders in surrender and looked me in the eyes.

Fine. Who do you need?

I couldn't help but smile as Kate reluctantly agreed to help me build a team. Running to hug her, she squeezed me tight for only a second before she released me and looked over my face sternly.

But you have to keep this quiet. If we're not careful, we could find out how well their biological weapons work. And not just us, everyone you involve. You're putting everyone's lives in danger if this doesn't work.

I know. But how many other lives would we be saving in the end?

Over the course of the next couple weeks, Kate and I approached the recruits we felt could be trusted and be useful to the plan. Every single person was unsure when the idea was first introduced. However, upon learning about what kind of research and projects the Society was attempting to hide, they seemed convinced that it should be done.

Brendan was, of course, the first recruit we approached. His access to the Society's system and database full of information made him a shoo-in for a part of the team. After all, it was his leak of information to Kate that shed light on the malevolent actions being done.

He sat on the firm gym mat, stretching his legs before classes began. When he heard the idea, his face paled and his eyes shifted around the room. Leaning forward, he mumbled under his breath.

You're crazy if you think that you can take down the Influencers. As soon as you try, they'll be knocking on your door.

So, you think it's impossible to take down their network?

Nothing is unable to be hacked but everything is traceable. There's no doubt they would trace it back to me if I ever tried anything.

We're not asking you to go in and start destroying everything now. Just study their system and try to find a weakness... some way to take it down. And permanently.

I can't promise anything but as soon as they get suspicious, I'm done.

Okay. But you'll help?

He looked back and forth between Kate's and my hopeful faces before grudgingly shaking his head.

I'll check it out. All I'm promising is that I'll look for a weakness.

That's all we ask, Brendan. Thank you so much.

He nodded, still shifting his eyes around the gym.

You guys are crazy, you know that?

Maybe. That might just be what it takes.

The second recruit that we introduced to the idea was Sam. His blueprints had ignited the plan into reality. After learning about who the Society really was, he immediately became motivated for the fight.

Heck, yeah. Let's take them down. What do you need from me?

Kate and I looked at one another, both surprised and pleased.

While we enjoy your enthusiasm, we do need to keep the plan under wraps. Don't tell anyone. Just us, okay?

You got it.

Sam's energy was still evident as he stood in the classroom where Kate and I had approached him. He shifted from one foot to the other as if he were about to join a football game or foot race.

You still got those blueprints?

He burst into motion, retreating to a cabinet with numerous blueprints stacked inside. After rummaging for a moment, he pulled it out and spread it across a classroom table. The three of us leaned over the blueprint, tracing lines and debating the best method.

The plan was coming together perfectly. Little did the Society know, we were using the knowledge that they provided to us to destroy them from the inside out. Until I could create a united plan that could absolutely succeed, the recruits only completed their research independently and reported back to me or Kate what they found.

Even Noah was involved in the planning. As Kate eased him into the idea of destroying the Society, he was adamant that we were wrong about them. He had been working with them for years. Yet, as Kate went on about our findings, his reality came crashing down.

I'm telling you: Brendan saw it with his own eyes. Countless files on, not only biological weapons, but bombs, laced vaccines, mass shootings, and terrorists. Everything they were created to stop, they are allowing to happen, actually causing.

So, you mean to tell me that I've been training people so the Society can use them for this? I've been helping them?

You didn't know, babe. It's okay.

Noah paused for a minute, absorbing the information that just turned his life upside down. Rubbing his back in comfort, Kate murmured reassurance into his ear. He shook his head in disbelief, finally looking to me in question.

Darcy, are you sure about this?

Absolutely.

And you think we can win?

I'm willing to risk it to find out.

I'm in. I'm done being in the dark and helping them to hide their true identity. Who else knows?

Kate and I walked him through our progress so far including the participation from Sam, Brendan, and Hannah.

Our team seemed to grow more and more each day, with new recruits and their unique skills coming into play. The plan fueled us in our training, both physically and mentally. Every one of us fought our hardest in the morning sessions, making it to the top of the bracket every time.

Ben seemed impressed with our improvement, raising his eyebrows in surprise as Brendan slammed a fellow classmate onto the mat with stealth. It was obvious that his victory had excited him as he walked around the boxing ring throwing his fists in the air.

Ben grinned at the previously quiet and rather unathletic, lanky boy strutting around the ring. He shook his head in amusement as he wrote down the results in his notebook.

Long after our afternoon classes were dismissed, each of us stayed behind and studied. As to not raise suspicion, we were careful about being in large groups or hovering around the blueprint for too long. If another person entered the room, we were merely a group of recruits talking after class.

Kate, Noah, and I spoke about nothing other than the Society over dinner every night. He proved to be an excellent source of knowledge when it came to the Influencers, from the chain of command to the shipment of goods that came through the tunnels.

It had to be the hardest that any of us worked since coming to the facility. There was a sense of unity, a common goal that drove us to improve. In the end, I didn't know what it was that fueled us most: our desire to stop the Society or the fear that they'd stop us first.

X.

SOLACE FROM THE COLD

Several guards joined the recruits surrounding the boxing ring in the gym one morning. Since the lessons had become more intense, we were held to higher standards in our abilities. This morning, Ben had informed us that we would be fighting one of the guards for our daily bracket. Only this time, the punishment was half an hour of running taken out of our lunch break.

Now, when you go up against the guards, know that your competitor is more experienced than you. Think through your moves because they'll be one step ahead of you at all times. But don't worry. Once a solid hit has been placed, the fight is over. Good luck, recruits.

Moments later, six guards walked through the door of the gym, arrogance and excitement dripping off them. Ben called the first recruit to the ring and let the guards choose among them who would accept the challenge.

Connor, of course, was the first to fight. He toyed with his recruit, a shorter Hispanic man who looked like he would be in his mid-twenties. Finally, after several failed jabs from the rookie, Connor placed a powerful hit to the side of his rib cage.

Ben ended the fight and called the next recruit up to the ring. It went like this until every guard had taken their turn. Connor competed with arrogance while Ben was strategic in his movements. It was fascinating to watch him dance around the ring. For being over six-foot-tall, he moved with great agility.

He was extremely strategic in every move, never hitting the recruit with full force. After their defeat, he would talk the recruits through what could have been done to prevent the hit.

Next, Kate was called to the ring and assigned a short, stocky guard not much taller than her. He approached her in the ring as if his work was already done. The bell echoed but he still risked a cocky grin over at his coworkers. Much to his surprise, Kate punched him in the face, stunning him and sending him stumbling backwards.

Kate wins record for the shortest fight of the day. Don't be too hurt, James. She's tougher than she looks.

Ben smiled as Kate bowed before her cheering audience, James giving him a glare out the corner of his eye in embarrassment.

Up next, Darcy Bishop.

The anticipation that had been building during the entire class fell on my chest like a ton of weights. I could already tell that Connor had been waiting for my turn, his face lighting up at the sound of my name.

He leaned into the circle of guards to decide my opponent. His eyes twinkled in delight as he stood to declare the fighter.

We choose Ben.

My stomach dropped as Ben and I simultaneously turned to one another in surprise. The guards started chanting his name to hurry his ascent to the ring where I stood. His eyes met mine, soft with despair. I shrugged my shoulders to signal that it was fine.

It's one hit.

Hesitantly, he got into position, hands held in defense and legs shoulder length apart. I approached him carefully, aware that he was extremely deliberate in every move. He dodged my first jab and blocked the second but didn't deliver a punch.

Again and again, I tried to find a weakness in his defense but failed every time. Not once did he make a serious attempt to strike me.

Stop pulling your punches, Ben. Just fight me.

He made a poor effort at a punch toward my ribs which I blocked with little effort. Anger was starting to well up inside of me, fueling my punches to become faster and harder. Noticing that I was no longer pulling my punches, Ben began to move quicker. However, his punches were still weak and poorly aimed.

Ben, hit me. Just do it. It's not a real fight.

His hits became harder but still held no real power. Blood rushed to my cheeks as I realized that he was enjoying my frustration. I could see a slight grin spreading across his face the angrier that I became. Adrenaline pushed me closer and closer to him, but he always managed to predict my moves.

I began to jab rapidly toward his torso, forcing him to place his forearms in front of him to block the punches. Suddenly, I saw my opening. As fast as I could, I jabbed toward his cheekbone, making sure to miss the nose.

The crowd of recruits cheered as they realized my victory. I stepped back from Ben in the ring and smiled from ear to ear. He rubbed his cheek and nodded to me in approval. A smile flashed across his face as he bowed in defeat to me, looking up with his green eyes twinkling in mischief.

The victory is yours.

I stalked off to the side of the ring, descending down to where Kate stood. Across the ring, I could see the satisfied grin on Connor's face as he watched Ben return to his place beside the platform. The rest of the recruits took their turn against the guards, with a large number of them having to give up a significant portion of their break.

After class was dismissed, I walked over to where Ben stood writing the results of the last fight in his notebook. He looked up at me when I was several feet away. I could see a slight redness where I had struck him on the cheekbone.

You pulled your punches.

What did you want me to do? Knock you out? You know Connor did that on purpose.

Yeah, I know… but I don't want you taking it easy on me. You didn't do that with any other recruit.

He paused and looked down at the floor.

No, I didn't.

The intensity in his eyes as he met my gaze showed the inner turmoil he faced in fighting me with the same force he used with the other recruits.

Well, next time, I won't take it easy on you either.

A deep chuckle rumbled in his throat as he looked down at me in amusement.

Oh, you took it easy on me, huh? So, what about this shiner I got from you?

Could've been a lot worse. I did try to avoid the nose. You seem like you would be a bleeder.

I laughed as I reached up and ran my finger along the redness of his cheekbone. His posture tensed as soon as I made contact. The pupils of his eyes were dilated, darkening them significantly. They were gentle as they looked down at me, studying my face.

You should really ice this.

I dropped my hand and watched as his soft gaze returned to his usual guarded expression. He nodded and picked up his jacket from the ground beside him.

Well, I'm going to go shower and eat lunch. I'll see you around, okay?

Okay. Good job today, Darcy. You've really been improving a lot lately.

Thanks.

I turned my back on him and walked out the gym, very aware of why I had improved. When the enemy is known, it's not difficult to fight harder and stronger. I didn't know if I could trust Ben, but I knew guilt was beginning to build inside me for keeping it from him.

After my shower, I grabbed a snack from the refrigerator before collapsing on my bed. Since classes had grown more intense, I found myself more exhausted each passing day. I rolled over on my side, looking at the clock. I should have already left for classes by now. I jumped out of bed, threw on my sandals, grabbed my textbooks, and ran out the door.

Hurrying down the hallway toward my first class, I heard someone say my name behind me. I turned to see Ben jogging up to me, hair still damp from his shower.

Hey, I've been looking for you. You running late?

Yeah, I passed out on my bed and just woke up a couple minutes ago.

Well, I better let you go then.

Oh, okay. Hey, do you want to have dinner at my place tonight? Kate and Noah will be there.

Yeah, sure.

Great. And that way, I won't be their third wheel.

He laughed and nodded toward my classroom door where the teacher could be heard starting the class. I ran off toward my door, looking back at him before entering the room. In a way, he seemed happier lately instead of burdened and reserved.

Standing in the hallway, it only seemed natural as he stood watching me go. His hands in the pockets of his jeans, he grinned toward me as I paused in front of the door. It no longer felt like a charade for Connor's benefit, but something both of us enjoyed.

In fact, when he showed up to dinner, I nearly forgot about where we were. It felt like four friends hanging out and having dinner together. He showed up as Kate was placing the pot of vegetable soup on the island with a loaf of crusty bread.

The aroma of the soup filled the apartment as she opened the lid. Ben and Noah were in the living area, talking amongst themselves while I sat and watched Kate dance around the kitchen. She always seemed so happy when she cooked for us.

Babe, that smells delicious. I'm starving.

Noah called from the living room, looking over the kitchen island at Kate as she placed the bowls and spoons at each place setting.

Well, it's ready, boys. Come and get it.

They stood up from their seats on the couch and made their way to the kitchen island. Around one corner of the counter, Kate had placed her and Noah with Ben and I sitting perpendicular to them.

Kate, this is amazing. Where did you learn to cook like this?

Growing up, I spent a lot of time in the kitchen with my mother and grandmother. They taught me everything I know.

Over our bowls of soup, all four of us shared stories about our lives. Kate and I both spoke about our mothers and what they taught us. Ben and Noah shared tales from working together for years, covering topics from extraordinary recruits to times Connor was hilariously put in his place.

At the end of the meal, Ben insisted that he help with the dishes. Sitting on the counter beside him, I watched as the soap bubbles clung to his hands and arms. I marveled at how he could make everything look so graceful, even the way he rinsed a bowl. I found my eyes lingering on his muscular forearms.

You know you don't have to do the dishes, right?

I know. Just thought it was the least I could do for you all providing dinner for me.

Ben finished rinsing all the dishes and had grabbed the kitchen towel to dry his hands. I jumped down from the counter and took the towel from his hands, beginning to dry the newly cleaned dishes.

It was no problem at all. We're glad you came.

Yeah, it was fun. Especially when Noah almost shot soup out his nose from laughing so hard.

He watched as I placed the last bowl in its rightful cabinet and threw the towel over the edge of the sink to dry. I gestured for him to follow me to the living room. He sat on the opposite end of the couch, moving the throw pillow out of his way.

I grabbed the blanket from the back of the couch and threw it over my chilled legs. My feet were dangerously close to touching his leg and I could feel the heat radiating from him.

How are you always so warm?

What do you mean always?

I mean I can always feel heat coming off you… in the hallway, the bed, now.

He looked surprised when I added "bed" to the list.

I didn't realize I was close enough for you to feel my body heat in bed.

I mean it's pretty easy to detect heat when you feel like an ice cube all the time. I get that from my mom. She was always cold.

Mine too. She could be wearing pants in the middle of the summer and still be chilled.

What were your parents like?

He sat in silence for a moment, contemplating whether he wanted to open up about his parents or not. Looking up to meet my gaze, I could see the vulnerability in his eyes. I could see the young boy who lost his parents.

They were great. My mom was gentle, patient, and compassionate. She lit up any room that she entered with her warmth. The kind of person everyone likes without her trying. My dad was passionate, focused, and smart. He could solve any equation you put in front of him. Together, they were unstoppable.

Ben gazed off in the distance, memories flashing through his mind.

They had taken me on many trips around the world: to peace conferences and cancer research center openings. But they refused for me to go on their last trip to South Sudan. I begged and begged to go but they wouldn't let me. They said it was too dangerous. Little did anyone know that would be the last time I saw them.

Tears welled up in my eyes as I pictured the young Ben finding out his parents were never coming back. I could tell the pain of that day had been one of the reasons he built walls around his emotions. If he built walls and didn't let others close, then he couldn't lose anyone.

He changed the topic, obviously not wanting to delve deeper into the topic of his parents. We talked about growing up, the places he'd been in the world, and the places we'd like to go.

I've always wanted to go to England. Not like Big Ben or anything. I want to go to places like Cornwall where the legends of King Arthur and the Knights of the Round Table took place.

Not the Bahamas or Jamaica?

He seemed amused by my nerdy preference for a vacation destination. His eyes twinkled as he looked over at me where I sat bundled under the blanket. I had since pushed my feet under his leg, warming the ice cubes that I called toes. The comfort his warmth provided me was indescribable.

We talked for hours until my eyes grew heavy and I fell asleep. In the midst of my sleep, I could feel Ben's arms around me as he lifted me off the couch and carried me down the hall to my bedroom.

Gently, he laid me down in the bed and placed the covers up to my shoulders. I could feel the brush of his fingers against my forehead as he pushed a stray strand of hair out of my face.

Falling in and out of sleep, I remember hearing him lay down on the other side of the bed before darkness consumed me once again. As with every night, my dreams were filled with death.

The church sanctuary where my mother's funeral took place was dark apart from a light above the casket at the front of the room. As I walked up to the coffin, I noticed that the church pews were empty.

Upon reaching the casket, I found that it was empty. I raised my head, searching the room for any sign of life. When my eyes returned to the empty silk pillow, I found that it was no longer vacant. Brendan lay pale as a ghost with blood splattered across his face. I continued my search for anyone else to ask questions, yet, found no one.

My dream became more disturbing when I realized that the face in the casket changed every time that I looked back down. The faces of my fellow recruits flashed before my eyes, stiff with their own mortality.

With each face, I grew more and more sure that it was my fault. The final face sent me into panic. Kate appeared in the casket, tiny in the large space. A single tear ran down her cheek. I heard her words echo in my head: *Darcy, it's a death wish. There's no way we could do it.*

The echoing words wouldn't stop, only growing louder and louder than before. I took several steps back from the casket, deafened by Kate's warning. But it was too late. It was my fault. They were dead because of me.

I couldn't breathe, couldn't stop the panic that overwhelmed me. My steps ceased as I slammed into the door at the back of the sanctuary with nowhere else to go. Then, I could hear another voice. It was no longer Kate's, but Ben's.

Darcy, wake up. You're okay. You're okay. Darcy.

My eyes opened and I was no longer in the church of my mother's funeral. The dim moonlight illuminated the wispy curtains above my bed and cast shadows on the furniture. I could feel Ben's hand leave my shoulder as I sat up.

Darcy, I'm sorry for waking you up but you were crying. Are you alright?

I shook my head, unable to find my voice. Wiping the tears that had run down my cheeks, I pulled my hair out of its tangled ponytail. There was no way that I would be able to sleep. With every blink of my eyes, a lifeless face of one of my friends appeared.

I heard the rustle of the bedding as Ben sat up to check on me. His eyes were filled with concern as he searched my face. I couldn't help but appreciate his presence after such an awful nightmare. My chest was heavy with the guilt of my friends' deaths.

It was just a nightmare. I'm fine.

He didn't seem persuaded as I turned to lay back down on my pillow. His head eventually landed back on his own pillow, brow still furrowed in worry.

Do you ever sleep through the entire night?

Rarely.

What was this dream about?

Losing more people that I love. And I couldn't stop it.

The room was silent. Not a single noise sounded through the entire flat.

When I lost my parents, I couldn't sleep either. I'd wake up in the night and feel so alone.

I realized I not only appreciated Ben being there but wanted him close. His warmth, the comfort he brought me, his scent; I wanted it all. Looking over at him, I noticed he had no guard up. It was just Ben. Ben with his soft eyes and ruffled hair curling over his temple.

I moved across the expanse between us and lay beside him. Our bodies touched; the warmth coming from his was overwhelmingly inviting. In the darkness of the room, I could make out the curve of his chest and the dip of his collarbone as his shirt pulled to one side. His eyes were both intense and skeptical as I came toward him.

Placing my body directly against his, I laid on my side and placed my head against his chest. He was tense at first, stiff as a board as I settled myself next to him. My hand on his chest, I could feel his heart rapidly beating. Gradually, his body relaxed and he wrapped his arm around my back, pulling me firmly against him.

We lay there, holding each other in the dark. Life had broken me to pieces at such a young age. Yet, there in that moment, he held all of my pieces, the uneven, shattered mess, together. It was my hope that I did that for him.

XI.

RENDEZVOUS WITH ME

From a deep sleep, I emerged fully refreshed. It was the most rested that I had felt in a long time. Blinking my eyes, I felt Ben breathing deeply under my hand. I raised my head to look at his face.

He was still sleeping, eyes shifting in a dream. I laid still and intently studied his features: his dark eyelashes, soft skin, sharp jawline, and tiny curls of hair around his temples. His chest was muscular, having provided a solid foundation on which to rest my head. During the night, he had placed his hands above his head allowing me to notice the bulge of his biceps and thickness of his forearms.

My examination of him was interrupted as he awoke, his eyes fluttering open. He raised his head and looked for me, grinning slightly when he found my eyes.

Good morning.

Morning.

Did you sleep any better after your nightmare?

Yes, thanks to you.

I'm glad I could help.

I sat up and stretched my arms in front of me. He stood up from the bed, still in his t-shirt and jeans from the night before. Slipping on his shoes, he looked out the window toward the horizon where the sunrise still colored the sand.

Darcy, what are we doing here?

Umm, getting out of bed.

No, you know what I mean.

Unsure of what to say, I looked down at my hands as I fidgeted with the soft material of the comforter. He turned around to look at me and I hesitantly met his eye contact. Soft eyes.

You're the one that showed up at my door. What do you think we're doing?

Since the first time I saw you that day in the gym, I've not been able to stay away from you. At first, I didn't want anyone else to have you. Not just Connor, any guard or recruit. I couldn't stop noticing you in classes, no matter how hard I tried to focus.

I got up from the bed and walked over to him. He glanced out the window, searching for words before looking back down at me.

Darcy, I can't get you out of my head. After my parents died, I shut everyone out. You're the only one that's managed to break through those walls I've built for so long. And I know this is the wrong place, time, and situation, but I like you Darcy. Actually, I'm crazy about you.

Ben...

He waited for the rest of my sentence, looking uncertain of my feelings.

I feel the same way.

His relief was apparent as he closed the gap between us and took me in his arms, not even giving me a chance to say more. I wrapped my arms around him as his lips met mine, firm at first and then softening into a passionate kiss. Melting into his arms, he tangled his hands in my hair.

When he broke away, his eyes were exploding with color. Though I had always called them green, a small amount of brown could be seen around the pupil up close. An incredulous smile spread across his face as he studied my expression.

You have no idea how long I've wanted to do that.

Why'd you wait so long?

He laughed and raised his eyebrows in amusement. His eyes flashed to the clock beside my bed, bringing a look of disappointment with it.

I've got to go get ready for class. I'll see you down there.

I nodded in agreement before he grabbed his shoes and walked out the bedroom door, glancing back at me before closing the door. After he left, I hurriedly got ready and went to the kitchen for a quick breakfast before class.

When I arrived at the gym, my circle of friends all had a similar look on their face. Every single face in the group was upset and concerned over presumably the same topic.

Kate, Brendan, Sam, and Hannah looked up at me as I arrived at their spot on the gym mat.

What? What's wrong?

Kate was the first to break the silence and gesture for me to come closer.

Darcy, Brendan found more projects that the Society is planning.

She looked to Brendan to explain further. He leaned in toward the middle of the group.

They're working on several mass shootings. Different locations and dates are being utilized to make it seem random and unplanned. They already have Society members assigned to do the killing.

When?

Scattered over the next couple of months.

We need to meet somewhere private to discuss the plan. It can't wait any longer. They're just hurting more and more people every day.

The circle of recruits all nodded in agreement. Kate looked to me for further direction.

And where do you propose we do that? We're kind of stuck here in their building. No place to really get away from them.

We'll just have to meet in our flat. Tonight, right after class. It will be early enough that they won't suspect anything other than friends hanging out.

Throughout lessons that day, I couldn't bring myself to focus. Over and over again, I ran the plan through my head: everyone's role and every action that had to be done. In the midst of my thoughts, I accidentally landed in the bottom of the bracket, earning my spot in an extra half an hour of running at the end of class.

Ben seemed to notice my absentmindedness as I started my run immediately after class. Upon offering me a quizzical expression, I merely shrugged my shoulders and continued my run.

Later in the hallway between classes, he questioned my subpar performance from earlier that morning.

You alright? You seemed like you were in another world this morning.

Yeah, I'm fine. Just distracted, I guess.

Well, I hope our conversation had nothing to do with it. I don't want to be a distraction or obstacle to your success.

No, it's not you. Believe me, if anything, you make living here like ten times better.

His infamous crooked grin flashed across his face as he leaned beside me on the wall. Although my statement was true, the guilt continued to build as I kept more and more secrets from him.

After the evening classes ended, I hurried back to the flat and waited for the other recruits to arrive. Kate and I sat in the living room, eager to begin the planning.

You really think this will work?

We can't afford not to try. There are innocent people dying out there because this Society thinks it's their job to decide everyone's fate.

I know, Darcy. But these people you've recruited to help with this crazy plan have lives that matter, too. I just want to be sure you know what you're risking.

Flashes of my nightmare from the night before ran through my mind. A chill went down my back as I looked over at Kate, seeming smaller and more vulnerable than ever before.

I know. And if something were to happen, I wouldn't be able to live with myself... but I also couldn't live with the fact that I did nothing. And someday, it might be us pulling the trigger. And then what?

A knock at the door sounded through the flat. Kate jumped up to answer it, finding Sam behind the door. Shortly after, Hannah and Brendan arrived. We all sat around the coffee table in the living area with a pen and paper to create visible plans.

First, I think we need to start the meeting by saying this is a dangerous mission. If you aren't willing to risk your safety to stop the Society, then I'll understand and leave you out of it.

Everyone looked around at each other, verifying participation. Once all eyes were on me again, I continued.

First things first: their electronic system. Brendan, is there any way to take it down? You had said before that they created it to prevent failure, but nothing is indestructible.

Actually, Darcy, I've been thinking. They have enough coding in their system that it would be impossible to find a script placed in the middle of it... unless they knew to look for it.

He seemed to be getting excited about his theory, sitting forward on the couch and moving his hands with each word.

I can create a script and plant it within all their coding. Its function will be to delete everything, almost like a black hole. My script will act as a worm, replicating itself until everything is destroyed.

And their firewalls and back-up servers?

As long as the script utilizes unblocked ports then it will work. And like I said, the worm will replicate until everything is gone, including back-up servers.

How long do we have until the script works?

I'm going to create it to only start working with a trigger. Once I pull the trigger, the entire system will be shut down while it deletes everything. The fire alarm, lights, and power will be disabled. They won't be able to turn it back on in time to stop the script.

Sounds perfect. Alright, Sam, have you studied the blueprints to the facility?

Yes, and I think I've identified the vital support beams. If we were to place explosives under those supports, then it would only be a matter of time before the entire place crumbles in on itself.

Hannah raised her hand in question as Sam explained his part of the plan.

And how do you suggest we find bombs here? It's not like they have TNT laying around for us to grab.

No, but they do have gas to fuel their generators and gun powder for their guns. Together, they would make a big enough explosion to take down a support column.

The plans were coming together with everyone collaborating and asking questions. Kate, with her chemistry and biology training, was able to help Sam with his idea on explosives.

Together, they were able to create a theoretical device that could be detonated based on a timer and planted in the columns before the shutdown.

Suddenly, I remembered Noah's lesson from the beginning of my time at the facility covering the institutions that make a business successful.

Guys, do you remember Noah's class about successful businesses? There were five institutions that enabled success: communication, information, leadership, funding, and...

Hannah jumped at the chance to use her training for the betterment of the team.

Manpower!

Right. So, Brendan is taking care of the communication and information with the system shut-down. I presume that empties their bank accounts as well?

Brendan nodded in confirmation before I continued.

So that means we still have to address manpower. Any ideas?

The room was silent while we thought of a way to disable their workforce. It was Brendan who spoke up first.

Now, I'm not promising anything but if I could figure out how to send a message to all the Society's members in the field before the system was destroyed, I could attach the files proving their malevolent activities. Hopefully, that would be enough to persuade most of them to stop their operations.

Hannah chimed in, seeming doubtful of Brendan's plan.

Yeah, it's a great plan but what if it doesn't stop them? What if they really are loyal to the Society, evil or not?

Well, that leaves us with our last topic: leadership. Without a leader, they won't have guidance or assignments.

I glanced over at Kate who seemed to have real doubts about the leadership part of the plan. Her brow was furrowed, seeming to be in inner turmoil.

Kate, Noah told you about the board members?

My question seemed to pull her out of her state of concern.

Uh, yeah. He said that there are six board members… and the President. The board members are able to vote but the President can overturn it if she wishes.

Sam inserted himself in the conversation, sitting on the edge of the couch.

And how exactly are you proposing on disabling leadership? Killing them?

No. Then we wouldn't be any better than them. No killing.

Then, I don't know how you expect to stop them. They'll just keep rebuilding if we don't stop them once and for all.

Maybe that part of the plan still needs some work and a lot more thought…

Placing the plan about leadership on the backburner for now, I stopped and looked at the notes and diagrams we had created on the paper in front of us. It was Hannah who asked the question of the hour.

So, we talked about an explosion, but how are we exactly planning on getting out of here?

The group broke out in laughter at how we overlooked a very essential part of the plan. Sam sobered up and reached for the paper where he had drawn a rough duplicate of the facility blueprints. He pointed near the bottom of the picture.

Here. There are tunnels leading to the outside world. The facility uses it for deployments and board member travel. With

Brendan being in IT, he should be able to gain access into their security system.

Actually, they designed that security system to be independent from all other systems. I don't have access to it, no one in IT does unless given special privileges from an executive member. They have key cards that allow them access.

So, you're saying that your system shutdown won't even affect the tunnels?

No. We need to have an access card.

Hannah interrupted the boys with yet another blunt observation.

Well, it looks like we're going to have to address leadership one way or another.

Suddenly, a knock sounded at the door. The recruits all looked around to see who was missing. Kate shook her head, narrowing the possibility that it could be Noah. She had wanted to keep Noah away from any suspicions that might occur from a guard gathering with a group of recruits outside of class.

I stood up and crossed the living room, opening the door. Outside stood Ben, wearing a hoodie and jeans. The surprise on my face must have been evident as he lingered outside of the door.

Is it a bad time?

Umm, no. Come on in.

He stepped through the doorway and immediately noticed the group of people in the living room. Sam nonchalantly grabbed the paper from the table, folding and placing it in his pocket. Kate's face paled as she saw Ben walk through the door.

Ben, how's it going? We just had some friends over to hang out.

Oh, cool. I didn't mean to interrupt. I can come back later.

No, we were actually about to call it a night.

Kate seemed rushed to excuse our meeting to Ben. She gave everyone a secret meaningful look as she stood up from the couch. They followed suit and said their goodbyes.

Luckily, Ben didn't seem to notice her odd behavior as he looked around the room at the other recruits. They filed through the open door and left Kate, Ben, and I alone in the doorway.

I really didn't mean to end your time together.

No, you're fine. We really were about done. We came straight from class so they're probably all hungry.

Okay, I'll see you in your room then.

As soon as he walked away, I looked at Kate.

What is your problem? You almost broke our cover by freaking out like you did.

I didn't freak out. I just quickly dismissed the group. We don't know who we can trust around here.

Yeah and what about Noah?

I trust Noah. Also, Noah isn't the head guard who has regular meetings with the Board and President.

Maybe, he could be useful then....

No, Darcy. Let's just limit the amount of people we involve, alright?

Shocked, I looked at her and searched for a reason for her guardedness. She wasn't making sense.

Well, I'm headed to bed. I'm exhausted. Night, Darcy.

I couldn't help but shake my head as she closed the door of her bedroom behind her. For some reason, she seemed adamant that Ben be excluded from the planning. Kate was essential to the plan and I couldn't chance losing her. Though I had my doubts, I decided it was best to follow her advice for now.

Before going to my bedroom, I went to the bathroom to wash my face. The splash of cold water on my cheeks felt refreshing after so much intense discussion. The logistics of the plan ran through my head as I searched for answers to the missing pieces.

I was in deep thought as I entered my bedroom, finding Ben looking out the window at the moon.

Almost a full moon, must mean the end of the month is here. Summer is coming fast.

His normal statement caught me off guard. Had I really been there that long?

Wait, what is today's date?

Let's see... May 31st. Why?

My birthday is June 2nd.

He seemed pleasantly surprised about learning another piece of personal information about me. I walked over to the window where he stood. Ben turned to pull me against his side with a grin on his face.

And I know just how to celebrate it.

Oh, you do? More lessons?

No. I'm going to cook dinner for you.

Are you a good cook?

He let out a chuckle as I questioned his abilities.

Good enough. You can come to my place.

His place? I had no idea I was even allowed to enter a guard's room. Trusting that Ben knew what he was doing, I nodded in agreement. Yawning, I made my way to the bed and collapsed on my side. The hunger that churned in my stomach was no match for the exhaustion that I felt from the long day.

I heard Ben chuckle at my graceful fall and felt the blankets as he pulled them over me. Suddenly, my head bounced on my pillow. He had collapsed on his side of the bed, mimicking me. His laughter was muffled by the pillow his face was buried in. I couldn't help but laugh as he rolled over and smiled at me.

He grabbed me and pulled me close to him, tucking me into his side. It wasn't long until his breathing slowed. However, my eyes refused to close. My mind was running in circles, about the plan, Kate, Ben, and my birthday.

I couldn't help but feel guilty about keeping Ben in the dark. He was the one person who I thought could make everything easier; the one person who I wanted to tell all my concerns and fears. After what seemed like an eternity of staring at the unending desert outside my window, thoughts turned into dreams as my eyes finally closed for the night.

XII.

ANOTHER YEAR OLDER

Memories of my past birthdays filled my head. Balloons, cake, my mother's smiling face. I remember rushing home from the last day of school giddy for the birthday celebration my mother had prepared.

Every year, she endeavored to make every birthday more and more special. As I ran in through the front door, I found colorful streamers and balloons littering the hallway.

I followed the decorations into the kitchen where my mother was placing the finishing touches on my birthday cake. The aroma of freshly baked cake wafted through the air, warm and sweet.

She smiled from ear to ear when she saw me standing in the doorway. Powdered sugar was scattered across the counter and part of her apron.

Happy Birthday, baby! I made your favorite: red velvet with cream cheese frosting.

I ran into the kitchen, hugging my mom around her waist. She squeezed me tight before bending down and offering me a taste from the icing bowl. My finger smeared the creamy white frosting across the glass of the bowl. A smile spread across her face as she witnessed my enjoyment of the finger full of sugar.

I was thinking that we could go to the movies tonight and watch that one you've been wanting to see. But first, dinner… and presents!

Countless other birthdays ran through my mind, drowning in images of my mother's face. But this year would be different. It would be the first year that I wouldn't have her here with me, the first birthday since she passed.

Though I knew my friends here in the Society would try their hardest to make it special, there would always be a vacancy where my mother should have been.

I awoke the morning of my birthday to my alarm clock. Looking beside me, I noticed that I was alone in the bed. Ben was nowhere to be seen. Slightly disappointed that he had left without saying goodbye, I started my normal morning routine.

Stepping into athletic capris and a tank top, I slid into tennis shoes and preceded to the bathroom. Looking in the dresser mirror at the tangled mess of my hair, I threw it up into a ponytail. When I opened the door, I was surprised to find Ben, Kate, and Noah standing outside my door. As soon as they saw me, they shouted, "Happy Birthday!"

They all smiled at my surprise, Kate in between the two boys who towered above her. In her hands was a plate of pancakes, topped with strawberries and whipped cream. I laughed in surprise as the three of them started singing *Happy Birthday* in unison, horribly out of tune.

Thanks, guys. That means a lot. You didn't have to make me breakfast.

Noah insisted that he make his pancakes for you again and I added the strawberries and whipped cream. It was all Ben's idea.

I smiled, making eye contact with every one of them. Kate was beaming with pride over her beautiful plating of pancakes. Noah smiled and nodded at me before his eyes were immediately drawn back to Kate. Finally, Ben's face was gentle as he looked down at me, his eyes sparkling with his beloved crooked grin.

Kate gestured for me to follow before she skipped off toward the kitchen. Noah chuckled at her enthusiasm and quickly followed after her, patting Ben's back as he passed him.

Making sure they were both around the corner, Ben turned his attention back to me. I stepped out into the hallway from the doorway of my bedroom.

Pulling his hands from his back pockets, he pulled me close to him and kissed my forehead. I wrapped my arms around his waist, looking up into his beautiful eyes.

Happy Birthday, Darcy.

Thank you. You didn't have to plan all of this.

I wanted to. I know it's not where you would've wanted to spend your birthday but then you wouldn't be with me.

Reaching on the tip of my toes, I placed my lips against his soft, warm mouth. Pulling me closer, he deepened the kiss until my head was light.

We pulled away from each other slowly as we heard Kate calling for us from down the hall. He merely smiled at me and grabbed my hand.

When I made these plans, I had no idea the amount of enthusiasm Kate would bring to the table.

I laughed and shook my head.

It wouldn't be Kate if not.

Allowing him to guide me to the kitchen, I found a large stack of pancakes, glasses of orange juice, and a bowl of strawberries placed in the middle of the island. Noah and Kate were seated, waiting for Ben and me to join them.

If you guys can pull yourself off of each other, breakfast is ready.

An ornery twinkle shined in Kate's eyes as she grinned mischievously over the counter toward us. I could see blood rush to Ben's cheeks as he pulled a chair out from the island for me.

Together, the four of us enjoyed the delicious pancakes, telling stories and laughing. I had nearly forgotten that we were in the facility of a secret society until Ben leaned over and kissed my cheek.

I have to go change before class. I'll see you down there.

You mean I still have to go to class?

I looked at him out the corner of my eye, waiting for his reaction to my joke.

Yes, and double the running for you.

Aww, it's what I've always wanted.

He put his plate in the sink and hollered over his shoulder as he walked toward the door.

You're welcome.

As the door clicked shut, Noah stood up and kissed Kate goodbye. He punched my arm softly as he went to leave. However, Kate seemed confused by his exit. Her brow was furrowed as she followed his journey to the door.

I thought you didn't have class until later in the morning.

No, I'm with you guys all morning. Ben switched it so that Connor was off today.

Looking down at my pancakes, I smiled to myself knowing fully that it was no coincidence. The day continued to be surprisingly amazing. Though I still had to attend classes, the friends I had made while here at the facility wished me Happy Birthday.

Every time I stole a glance at Ben, he would look at me and smile. The Ben who I met, the guarded, stoic leader, had become my comfort, happiness, and protector. When he shared another piece of himself with me, I couldn't help but fall a little bit harder for him.

He walked me to my flat after class, holding my hand tenderly. Stopping outside of my door, he leaned over and kissed me quickly on the lips.

Are you looking forward to your birthday dinner tonight?

Yes. May I ask what gourmet meal you have planned for us?

It's a surprise.

It's macaroni and cheese, isn't it?

Oh, ye of little faith. Don't you think I can do more than throw a box of noodles in some water?

I'll answer that after supper tonight.

Shaking his head, he laughed at my lack of faith in his cooking. Since I was drenched in sweat from that morning's training, I excused myself to go shower.

I'm dying to get this sweat off me.

Alright, I'll see you tonight after your classes.

Nodding, I pushed the door of the flat open. Kate had already finished with her shower, walking down the hallway in her towel.

Hey, Darcy. I was thinking that I could help you get ready for your date with Ben tonight. There's a curling iron and some makeup in the bathroom.

Do I really look that bad?

Well, right now you're a sweaty mess…

She scrunched her nose and pretended to fan away my stench.

No, you're beautiful exactly how you are. I just wanted to do something nice for you.

Okay. But not too much. I've never been much for a lot of makeup.

She clapped her hands in excitement and ran into her bedroom to get dressed. I immediately went to the bathroom, shedding off the drenched clothes and throwing them on the ground. Turning the temperature cooler, I stepped in the shower and cleansed myself of what felt like five layers of sweat.

After I dried off with one of our big, soft towels, I headed back toward my room. The soft padding of my feet against the hardwood floors resounded through the hall.

Throwing on a pair of jeans and blouse for classes, I went to the refrigerator for a bottle of water. The pancakes still filled my stomach from that morning, leaving no desire for lunch.

I couldn't get my mind off Ben. In the past month of spending every night with him, we had learned so much about one another. We had shared our likes and dislikes as well as stories about our parents and childhoods. He was the person who knew the most about me since my mother, including Kate.

So why did I feel so nervous to be alone with him tonight? We had slept in the same bed for nearly a month… but Kate and Noah had always been across the hall.

As each afternoon class ended, the anticipation of my birthday dinner only increased. When we got back to the flat from our lessons, Kate pulled me into the bathroom with her and heated up the curling iron. Her hands were gentle as she pulled bunches of my hair up, wrapping it around the styling wand.

So, what is Ben cooking for you this evening?

I don't know. He wouldn't tell me.

Well, can he cook?

He claimed "good enough."

Kate laughed and rubbed my back in reassurance. She met eye contact with me in the mirror, smiling.

I'll save you some dinner tonight if you're hungry when you get back.

She placed the curling iron on the bathroom counter and ran her hands through the new curls to loosen them. Kate was very skilled with styling hair, the soft beach waves cascading down my back. Opening one of the drawers, she grabbed a pouch and emptied its contents into the sink.

Bottles of foundation, concealer, eye shadow, mascara, eyeliner, and lip gloss filled the bottom of the sink. She lifted my chin up with her fingers and began gently applying the foundation. Soon she had moved onto the eye makeup and finally the lips.

Moving from between the mirror and I, Kate stood back and looked at her work. I looked in the mirror, pleasantly surprised by her effort. Afraid that I would look like a poodle with tight curls, I was delighted by the loose curls she had achieved.

Kate, knowing I was not much for a lot of makeup, created a natural glow with the foundation and neutral eye shadow. The cherry on top, light pink lip gloss finished the entire look.

You look so pretty!

Thanks, Kate. You did an awesome job.

Okay, go get dressed. He'll be here any moment.

She hurried me out of the bathroom, pushing me through the doorway of my bedroom. Opening my closet, I found several dresses. I chose a mid-length summer dress. The white material was woven around the bodice until the waistline where pastel yellow chiffon flowed just below my knees.

Throwing the dress on the bed, I shed my classroom clothes and dropped them on the floor. Opening the top drawers of the dresser, I found bras and panties. I looked at myself in the mirror, standing only in my cotton bra and underwear. Hesitantly, I returned my attention back to the drawer of lace.

I raised my eyebrows in surprise at the number of high-quality undergarments the Society provided to their recruits. Settling in the middle of the extremes, I chose a pair of silky panties and a lacey bra that would not be seen with the cut of my dress.

After I had stepped into the dress, I looked at the reflection of myself. Since coming to the facility, my arms and legs had toned from the daily exercise and my hair had grown slightly longer. In my posture, there was confidence, a surety that I could protect myself.

Kate knocked at the door as I stepped into a pair of sandals, sucking in breath as soon as she opened the door.

Oh, Darcy, I love that dress! And I just wanted to let you know... Ben is here.

Oh, okay. I'll be right out.

The click of the door sounded behind her. With one more look in the mirror, I went out into the hallway and walked toward the kitchen. Kate was nowhere to be seen, respectfully giving us privacy.

There stood Ben near the entry of the flat, in dark jeans and a navy-blue button-down shirt. His hair had been trimmed slightly to tame the curls that occurred on the ends. As he looked up at the sound of my feet, a look of astonishment flashed across his face.

Darcy, you look so beautiful.

Well, thank you. You don't look too bad yourself.

He looked down at his outfit, unpersuaded by my comment. Opening the door, he held his hand to lead me through the doorway and out into the hallway. Our hands intertwined as he led me to the elevators.

As the doors slid closed, he pressed the button for the second floor. He looked down at me, his green eyes soft.

Have you had a good birthday so far?

Yes. You all have been very kind.

I would've brought you flowers but we're kind of in the middle of a desert in a locked down facility.

Yeah, I understand.

Chuckling, I thought of the distance between us and the nearest flower, the distance from home.

What is your favorite flower?

Blue hydrangeas.

Hmm. I'll have to remember that.

It was my mother's favorite flower. She always said they reminded her of my father's eyes.

Of your eyes.

Yes.

The elevator door opened to the second floor of the facility where the guards lived. There was no difference in the appearance of the hallway as we turned to the right immediately out of the elevator. His room was on the left side of the hall at the very end.

Certain I heard someone behind us, I turned around to find no sign of life. The hallway was empty, and I turned my attention back to Ben. Pulling a set of keys from his pocket, he unlocked the door and held his hand to invite me inside.

As I walked through the door, I saw that his apartment was indeed half the size of Kate's and mine. However, it was still skillfully decorated with a large room near the entrance comprising the kitchen and living area. A set of couches made of black leather were placed on the right side of the room.

Then, my eyes fell upon the kitchen. There on the island counter were lit candles, illuminating the plates and glasses that he had placed carefully for the two of us. A large pot sat in between the two plates, most likely the source of the delicious scent wafting in the air.

I heard the door close behind me and felt Ben's hand on the small of my back.

I hope it's good. Macaroni and cheese is challenging.

He looked at me out of the corner of his eye, waiting for my reaction. I laughed and let him guide me to my chair. Before he sat in his own chair, he opened the pot to reveal roasted chicken over a bed of rice and vegetables.

Wow. That looks delicious.

Thank you. With a limited amount of ingredients and skill, this is the best I could do.

He filled our plates and then sat in his chair. I picked up the fork next to my plate and brought a piece of carrot to my mouth.

It's very good, Ben. Thank you.

It's the least I could do for your birthday. So, tell me about your birthdays growing up. Big parties?

No, actually. It was just me and my mom. She would always make me a cake and plan something. One year, we went to the movies. Another year, we went on vacation to California.

It seemed to dawn on him all at once. His face grew somber in the soft candlelight.

This is your first birthday without your mom. Oh, Darcy, I'm so sorry.

I nodded, unable to speak as tears caught in my throat. It was all I could do not to cry as Ben's hand wrapped around my own. We continued to eat our dinner, talking of lighter topics: favorite cakes, childhood gifts, places to vacation.

He cleared the dinner from the counter when we had both finished. Inviting me to the couch, he presented me with a small gift wrapped in paper. With no stores within miles, I was shocked to see him with a gift. He grinned at me as he offered me the small box.

Slowly, I took the box out of his hand and removed the paper from the outside. There was a small red box beneath the casing. Lifting the lid of the box, I drew in breath at the sight of a beautiful necklace. It was simple and elegant, the silver chain leading to a small circle of diamonds. In the center of the circle sat a single white pearl.

It was my mother's.

Holding the necklace in my hands, I gasped at his confession.

Ben, I couldn't possibly take something that was your mother's. I'm sorry. I just can't accept this.

I put the necklace carefully back in the box and tried to hand it back to him. He took the box and opened it, grabbing the jewelry and unclasping the chain.

He stood up and disappeared behind me. Gently, he grabbed my hair and pushed it to side. I felt the cold metal of the necklace against the skin on my chest. Ben came back into view, studying the necklace on me.

Perfect.

Ben, I can't take your mother's necklace.

I want you to have it. She would have liked you.

My hand went to the pearl, feeling the roughness of the diamonds around it.

Thank you, Ben. It's beautiful.

Happy Birthday, Darcy.

His eyes were like a burst of color, an explosion of green and brown. There was no sign of defense in them, no guard or wall built to keep me out.

Ben, when we first met, you were so guarded. But now…

The day my parents died, I was left alone in the world. I was fourteen at the time, so I was placed with my nearest relative. My aunt, she was a very stern woman. She distrusted everyone, even her own family, and taught me to do the same thing. If I built walls, no one could hurt me.

Your aunt sounds awful.

She had her moments. Though she had a tough exterior, she was still fiercely protective of those who managed to become close to her. When I had nothing, she took me in.

But to teach a fourteen-year-old to distance himself from the world sounds terrible. You get lonely behind those walls.

Yes, you do. But then I found you.

It was the punch to the face that won you over, wasn't it? You're afraid I'll do it again.

He let out a deep chuckle and looked into my eyes.

No, it wasn't the punch. But thanks for bringing it up again. I just now managed to forget it.

It was then that Ben grew very serious. He leaned toward me, taking my hands in his and maintained eye contact.

Darcy, there's something I've wanted to tell you for some time, but I couldn't bring myself to say it until now.

I waited for him to continue. It obvious that he was heavily burdened with the information.

Out of all the recruits I have trained, there has never been anyone like you. From the first time I laid eyes on you, I couldn't take them off. You are the first person I want to see in the morning and the last touch I want on my skin at night. From the first day I met you, you have torn down all of my walls with a single look, single touch, single kiss. Darcy, I love you.

You love me?

Yes. I always have. I just wouldn't admit it to myself. My aunt taught me that love makes you weak, but I've never felt stronger.

Ironically, I'd never felt weaker in the knees. His intensity as he spoke was overwhelming. I could feel the warmth of his body close to mine, see the heartbeat in his neck.

I looked down at his hands clutching mine. Any words I could have possibly thought in that moment managed to get lost before reaching my mouth.

Did I know what love was? Was it my mother never finding another after she lost my dad or the cheesy lines said in movies? I had always wondered if I would know what it was when I felt it. Countless love songs, poems, and movies attempted to put it into words. Love was so much more than words could ever describe.

The depth of feelings, longing for a person. The willingness to sacrifice anything and everything for their happiness. Every tiny characteristic that made them who they were. Never able to spend enough time with them, never being complete without them. One word but so much more: Love.

I hadn't realized the doubt that had appeared on Ben's face as he waited for my response. In that moment, it didn't matter the number of words in the English language, in any language. There were only three words that could encompass the fathomless feelings I felt for Ben.

But it was too late, Ben had his guard back up. I had waited too long to speak. He thought he had crossed a line and made me uncomfortable. Standing up, he paced toward the door.

I'm sorry. I didn't mean to scare you. I'll take you back to your room now and leave you alone for the night.

Ben...

He began to open the door, unwilling to look me in the face. I jumped up and ran over to the door, shutting it the little bit that he had opened it.

Ben, would you wait a second? Stop pushing me away.

He looked down at me, vulnerable and hurt. The anticipation of the moment only seemed to build his doubt.

It was a mistake, okay? Let's just forget about it.

My heart ached as he so quickly tried to dismiss his declaration. The time to share my feelings was closing as his stoic demeanor began its inevitable return.

Would you stop for a second? Can't you see that I love you?

Then, his lips were on mine. There was a desperateness in his kiss. I threw my arms around his neck as he gently pushed me against the door. His body was pressed firmly against mine, but it still didn't seem close enough.

My hands ran down his back and over his chest while his were tangled in my hair. His lips moved from mine down my neck, his tongue grazing my skin softly. Ben's hands had moved from my hair to my back where my dress opened into straps.

His lips returning to mine, the kisses were deeper than they had ever been. My head had gotten light with all the excitement, but I couldn't stop. I wanted him close, needed it. And he seemed to need it, too.

My hands gradually moved from his back to his beltline, caressing his skin beneath the waistband. His eyes opened quickly as he gasped in surprise. He looked into my eyes, both of us breathless.

Darcy, we don't have to…

I know, but I want to.

He seemed to weigh out the decision.

Are you sure?

I pressed my lips firmly against his and pulled him by his belt closer to me. It was then that Ben stopped holding back, his hands became more sure, his lips hungrier. He picked me up and starting walking down the hallway behind his kitchen.

Ben walked through the doorway of his bedroom, still kissing me as my feet dangled. He put me down next to the bed and looked at me for final approval. His chest moved quickly with excitement, but his eyes took the time to assess my comfort. I reached for the buttons of his shirt, undoing them one by one until his bare chest was visible.

I ran my hands up his chest to his arms, pushing the sleeves off his biceps and letting the shirt hit the floor. He watched me as I stood, studying his shirtless body. The muscles were defined all along his torso, creating indentations along his abdomen and ribs.

Ben came closer to me, grabbing my dress and pulling it over my head. Our clothes had become scattered along the floor. I sat on the bed and pulled him on top of me. His hands ran along my body: my back and chest then my thighs and legs.

Desperately, I fiddled with the button of his jeans until I was successful in opening them. Then, it was only us in the bed. He hovered over me, his intense green eyes watching me in between kisses. I wanted to give him everything, every part of my body, soul, and mind. It was all his and he was all mine.

I had never wanted anything, anyone so much in my life. The desire was overwhelming. It was as if the entire world stopped for us. In that moment, it was only Ben and me. There was no facility, no secret society. Only us.

XIII.

BED CHECK

In the morning, I woke up to Ben's bare chest beneath my head. We were wrapped around each other under the covers of his bed. As he felt me stir, he opened his eyes and kissed my forehead.

Good morning, my love.

Good morning.

He turned on his side and placed his hand under my chin, tilting my mouth to meet his. Pulling away slowly, he pushed my hair behind my ear and grazed my cheek softly. His eyes were tender as he studied my face. Grinning up at him, I suddenly remembered our mandatory morning schedule.

What time is it? I should probably get ready for class. Plus, Kate's probably worried about me since I didn't come home last night.

I jumped out of bed and found my dress, pulling it over my head. He had gotten out of bed and was pulling on his jeans from the night before. Suddenly, a loud knock echoed from the door.

Ben was alert. It was obvious that he didn't get visitors much. He tensed up, throwing on a t-shirt before heading toward the bedroom door.

Stay here.

My heart beat hard in my chest, confused about what was going on. He cracked the door behind him. I could hear his feet hit the floor until his apartment door opened.

Can I help you?

We know that Darcy Bishop is here. Please have her come out now.

I stepped out into the hallway, Ben looking up desperately at me from the door where several guards stood. The guards immediately noticed my presence and walked toward me. With a guard on each arm, they began to force me toward the door.

Hold on. What are you doing to her? There were no rules broken here.

Each recruit must be in their assigned apartment by eleven at night. The President would like to see Darcy in her office for her punishment.

Punishment? Guards and recruits stay the night with each other all the time.

Yes, but never in the guard's quarters. It is prohibited.

Their strong grasp could not be broken as they walked me out of Ben's apartment to the elevator. As we passed several doors on the way to the elevator, one opened abruptly to reveal Connor.

His smug smile said it all. He had been the one I heard last night in the hallway, the one who reported me to the President. I glared at him as the guards continued to push me toward the elevator.

They guided me through the facility until we reached the same executive hallway that Stanley guided me down on my first day here. Except now, I saw through the fancy décor to the malevolent mission of the Society. The hidden poison in their flower arrangements, the pretense behind their beautiful paintings.

The hallway was eerily silent as they pushed me toward the President's office door. As the door opened, I could see the sunrise coming through the windows. The natural light illuminated the office, casting small shadows along the desk and chairs.

Margot Clarke sat upright in her chair, looking down at papers on her desk. When she heard the knock at the door, she looked up over her reading glasses. Immediately, she dropped the papers on her desk and watched as the guards seated me in front of her.

If she had been stern before, today she was on a whole new level. The chill coming from her could be felt across the space between us. The door clicked shut behind the guards before the President chose to speak.

Darcy Bishop, I was made aware that you were not in your assigned flat last night. Apparently, you were not informed of the curfew placed on all recruits. May I ask you where you stayed?

I think you know where I stayed. That's why I am here.

If you are wise, you will answer my questions quickly and truthfully.

Her sharp and cold tone seemed to hold a threat. I maintained eye contact over her desk and grinded my teeth.

I stayed the night with Ben Lewis.

Yes, Ben seems to be quite infatuated with you. Although, I have no idea why.

I'm sorry but I don't see how your opinion of my personal relationships matters. I'm here against my will. I'm training for your missions. What more do you want from me? To be a robot and have no feelings like you?

Margot's eyes became fierce in reaction to my blunt admission. She leaned forward in her chair and spoke through pursed lips.

I would be careful what you say to me, Miss Bishop.

Why should I care? What's left to be done? You took me out of my own home. All because I had no one to miss me, no one to come looking for me. So, before you go threatening your recruits, make sure they have something to lose, something you haven't already taken from them.

A wicked grin spread across her face. If I had thought her demeanor could be any more spine chilling than before, she proved me wrong.

There is always more to lose. Trust me.

As if you know me well enough.

I think my nephew would have another opinion on that, my dear.

Your nephew?

Then, it hit me. Ben's stern aunt who taught him not to trust anyone. The aunt who took care of him after his parents died, who taught a fourteen-year-old boy to build walls so that no one could hurt him; the one who was fiercely protective of her few loved ones. And it seemed as though I had become involved with one of those few people.

Ben is your nephew?

Yes. I tried to tell him not to become involved with you. I've known from the start that you have a rebellious spirit. Yet, his infatuation with you overwhelmed his common sense.

I sat stunned at her confession. Of all the people who I could have fallen in love with, why did it have to be the nephew of the President of the Society that I was planning to destroy?

She sat, seeming pleased with the shock evident across my face. Leaning back in her seat, she crossed her legs and placed her hands in her lap. Then, her eyes were drawn toward my chest, focusing on the necklace. The tension emanated from her body and her eyes were like daggers. She gulped back her fury before proceeding through gritted teeth.

Now, for the curfew that you have broken, there must be punishment. However, nothing comes to mind that is quite fitting of your behavior. I will have to request your presence again once I decide what I would like to do with you.

The lack of immediate consequences surprised me.

You may leave now. The guards will see you out.

With a press of a button, the guards who had first dragged me there opened the door and ushered me out of her office. She held a haughty smirk as I looked back at her. She called my bluff. She knew I had something left to lose and now she planned to take more. Not only that, but she was savoring the pleasure she felt as she punished me.

The guards guided me back through the executive hall and released me as soon as we exited the elevator. Still in the dress from the night before with my hair knotted and makeup smeared, I made my way quickly back to my flat hoping to avoid being seen by anyone on the way.

Once the elevator made it to the fifth floor, I turned toward the flat Kate and I shared. Much to my despair, sitting on the floor outside the door was Ben. He had his knees drawn up and his arms crossed on top of them, laying his head on his forearms.

When he heard me approach, he looked up and jumped to his feet. He started toward me but stopped in his tracks the moment he saw the expression on my face.

Darcy, what's wrong?

I stood there, the fury I felt for Margot building up in my veins. The anger took over my emotions and fueled the words to flow out of my mouth.

You're her nephew?!?

His face paled as I confronted him.

You didn't think that was something I should've known? Something you should've thought about when you became involved with me?

Darcy...

Why didn't you tell me, Ben? Of all those things we told each other, you couldn't tell me that the President of the Society was your aunt?

He still stood motionless, struggling to get a word in between mine. His hands hung motionless at his sides.

Last night, you even told me about how your aunt raised you and you didn't think to say, "and oh, yeah, she's the President." As if she didn't hate me enough, now I've had sex with her nephew!

Darcy...

I trusted you, Ben. And now, only God knows what punishment she's going to choose for the harlot who defiled her nephew!

Darcy, calm down. Let's go somewhere private and I'll explain everything.

No. There's nothing to explain. It's all very clear to me now.

I pushed past him toward the door to my apartment. His hand grabbed my elbow in protest. Spinning around, I viciously ripped my arm from his grasp.

I trusted you.

I don't see how this changes anything. You didn't fall in love with the nephew of the President, you fell in love with me. None of this matters. Darcy, this doesn't change anything between us.

You don't know, do you?

His furrowed eyebrows only added to the confusion already running across his face.

What don't I know?

The Society your parents created isn't what you think it is. You're sheltered here in the facility, with your aunt making sure nothing gets to you or anyone else.

What are you talking about?

They're not curing disease and fighting for world peace, Ben. Actually, they are doing the exact opposite. Biological weapons, mass shootings, plagues, war. You name it, they're involved.

How would you even know any of this? You're here just like me.

*Like I would tell you where I got the information. You'll
just run to your aunt and get them punished, too.*

*No, you're wrong. Darcy, you're upset. Just calm down.
You don't know what you're talking about.*

I shook my head in disbelief, my mouth gaping in
astonishment. He seemed unaware of what had just dawned on
me.

*You're one of them. You've been on their side from the
start.*

There are no sides. We're all a part of this.

*No, I'm not. I will never be. They're murderers disguised
as a benevolent government... and you're helping them.*

*My parents were not murderers. They created this group
for good. I don't believe you.*

*It might have been created for good, but it's no longer run
by the same people. Your aunt is not what she seems.*

Darcy, stop. You're wrong.

*It doesn't matter anymore, does it? Whatever punishment
your aunt chooses for me will likely put space in between you and
me.*

*I'll talk to her. It was my fault that you weren't in your flat
by curfew.*

*It won't matter. She'll tell you what you want to hear and
make her own decisions about me either way.*

Please, Darcy. Let me try.

173

It's over, Ben. I can't trust you.

He tried once again to grab my arm, the heat of his hand running electricity across my skin. Fighting the urge to welcome his touch, I pulled my arm away and opened the door to my flat without a glance back.

Slamming the door behind me, I looked around the open apartment. There Kate stood in the hallway, still in her pajamas. Her eyes were as big as saucers as she looked me over from head to toe.

Darcy?

As soon as I heard her soft voice, I crumpled to the floor right in front of the door. My sobs came from the deepest part of my soul, shaking my chest to its core. I heard the patter of her bare feet come across the floor to where I sat.

Darcy! What happened?

The sobs left no room for words as I struggled for breath.

Say something, Darcy.

He's her nephew. The President's nephew.

Kate fell silent. The hand that rubbed my back grew still. My sobs had subsided enough to notice her odd behavior. I looked up at her face, now still and filled with regret.

I stood up and looked down at her still crouching, realizing why she had become silent.

You knew. You knew he was her nephew and you didn't tell me. Am I the only one who didn't know?

Noah told me. I'm so sorry I didn't tell you, Darcy.

And that's why you didn't want me to tell him about the plan.

Yes. But, Darcy, you have to understand, he's not his aunt. None of us were trying to hurt you. You fell in love with him, not his aunt.

Unknowingly, she had quoted Ben's exact statement from the hallway.

How could I love someone who is a part of this Society?

We're all a part of it now, babe.

Not for long.

What do you mean? Darcy, don't do anything stupid.

The plan just needs a few more details figured out. It has to happen soon.

You can't let your emotions control this plan. That will ruin everything. You need to have a clear head and the right timing.

I know. Today has only motivated me to make it better. We won't fail. I'll die before that happens.

Her face had grown heavy with concern. I was halfway to my bedroom before she decided to reply.

It's not just your life you're risking. All of us are involved.

I whirled around and met eye contact with her, unblinkingly.

But how many more lives do they have to ruin before we do something?

Turning back around, I finished the trek down the hall to my room. Shutting the door firmly behind me, I stripped off the dress from the night before. I could still smell Ben on the front of it. Throwing it across the room in frustration, I threw my hair up in a ponytail to get it out of my face.

Looking at the clock, I hurriedly changed into sports apparel and headed to the bathroom. Grabbing a washcloth from the bathroom cabinet, I washed the remaining makeup from my face. In my fury, it felt as though I had rubbed the first three layers of skin from my face.

I caught a glance of myself in the mirror. I didn't recognize the girl that looked back at me. Vengeance filled her eyes. The blue no longer the color of flowers but of the ocean, powerful enough to sweep away even the strongest of cities, the highest of mountains.

The vacation when my mother took me to California ran through my head. I remember standing on the edge of the beach, looking out at the ocean. I couldn't help but be humbled by its size. Me, one tiny spot in the existence of time, standing beside something so powerful, so everlasting.

With one small wave, it could mark me from existence. No one would find me, forever lost in its vastness, its depths, its darkness.

I vowed to myself that I would wash the Influencers off the face of the earth. They would no longer play God, choosing when and where people should die. As humans, we had no right to make that decision.

Heading down to that day's lessons, I walked at a quick pace, ablaze with anger. Ben still hadn't showed up whenever I arrived, only the recruits and Noah.

Noah looked at his watch and then around the room for any sign of him. Finally, he told the recruits to start with their daily run. I ran next to Kate, both of us silent. As we finished with our laps and paired up for warm-ups, the gym door slammed. Ben strode into the room in the usual athletic shorts and t-shirt.

I refused to watch him as he approached Noah, keeping my eyes on Kate as she threw the medicine ball back to me. Carefully, she threw the ball back into my arms, aware that my attention was not totally on her.

However, I couldn't keep my eyes from him for long. Ben stood by Noah, most likely apologizing for his tardiness. Then, he turned and watched the recruits complete their warm-up exercises together. Quickly, I turned my head away from him before he noticed my stare.

I hated that I was still attracted to him, every move, every touch, every word. I still loved him even when I shouldn't have.

After warm-ups were done, Ben took over with the normal course of lessons. Oddly enough, the entire day went by as usual.

Morning classes, lunch break, afternoon classes. The only thing missing was Ben, who I avoided like the plague. He didn't seem too convinced that he wanted to approach me quite yet either, acting as if I blended with the other recruits.

He avoided eye contact, keeping his head down whenever I came close. It was not an act of fear, but out of loss for words. I wondered if he had the same aching hole in his chest that I constantly felt.

But I couldn't succumb to the pain, to the gut-wrenching emptiness I felt when I laid in bed alone at night and woke up without him there. When I turned to share a joke with him and found emptiness. Dreaming about his touch and waking up to the painful reality of his permanent absence. I couldn't love him. Loving him would be loving a part of the Society, the Society that I pledged to destroy. Or die trying.

XIV.

BLOODY CONSEQUENCES

It had been two days since my meeting with Margot, since she promised to choose a punishment fitting of the crime. Knowing that I had gotten involved with her nephew, the punishment would doubtlessly surpass the crime.

Every morning, I watched the gym door for the guards to take me away. And every day, they didn't come. I couldn't help but notice that Ben was not looking at the door.

On the morning of the third day, I approached him before class. He seemed surprised by my arrival, guard up yet again. His eyes a shield that could block any slur of harmful words.

Darcy.

You talked to her, didn't you? That's why I haven't heard from her.

Yes, I did.

Why did you do that? Just let it happen. I'm not yours to protect anymore.

His eyes darkened with intensity. He opened his mouth to say something but was interrupted. Unexpectedly, a chuckle echoed behind us. I turned to find Connor, clapping his hands in applause.

Wonderful! The two love birds are out of the honeymoon phase! What could've happened that has caused this tension?

The fury that had been building for days no longer allowed me to ignore Connor. My words flew out in a slur of anger as I whirled to face him.

You know exactly what happened, Connor. You're a snitch.

Ben came around from behind me, confused by our conversation. His brow was furrowed in uncertainty, looking between the two of us.

Wait, what's going on?

Your partner, Connor, is the one that told your aunt about us. I heard him in the hallway that night and saw him in the morning looking like he just won a fight.

Ben turned his attention to Connor, looking at him in disbelief.

You're the one who told her? This is none of your business, Connor. What I tell my aunt and who I spend my time with is my business.

I have no idea what you're talking about, Ben.

His act of innocence was too much for me. I had enough of his games. As I lunged toward him furiously, Ben stepped in between and caught me in midair. My legs kicked as he picked me up and placed me several steps away. Connor merely looked amused by the display.

You should really get a leash for her.

I looked up at Ben, feeling him tense up at Connor's comment. He looked down at me, his eyes burning with rage. A sense of dread came over me as I looked up at his face, never before seeing such unbridled anger.

Before I could calm him, he let me go and whirled around to Connor. In a flash, Ben had punched Connor in the nose, hard enough to make him bend over in agony.

Connor, blood flooding out of his nose, looked up at Ben before hurling toward him. Ben quickly absorbed the tackle and threw a knee into Connor's ribs. I could hear the wind escape his lungs in a gush as Ben's unrestrained hit struck hard. By the time Connor had gotten back up for another round, there were two guards in the gym waiting for class to start who intervened.

With a guard on each side, Connor was held back from Ben who stood with fists clenched. He spit blood from his mouth as he hurled words in Ben's direction.

You'll pay for this. Auntie can't protect you from me forever.

Ben gestured for the guards to take him out of the gym. The recruits had stopped their conversations and were watching the entire event with their eyes wide open and mouths gaped. He turned around and looked at me. Connor's blood had stained the front of his white shirt. His eyes showed a mix of emotions: fury, regret, longing, sorrow.

Ben walked to the front of the class and ordered the recruits to run their laps. Looking back at him, I hesitantly began my run next to Kate. She touched my arm gently to let me know she was there for me. With a nod, I let her know I appreciated her.

Near the end of the morning lessons, two guards walked into the gym and approached Ben. He dropped his head and nodded in agreement. Looking up, his eyes searched across the expanse of the gym, finally falling upon me. They were filled with remorse and anxiety.

Alright, recruits. That's enough for today. Go to lunch.

In their small groups, the recruits filed out of the gym.

Darcy, could you come here please?

My heart dropped. It wasn't him they wanted; it was me. Ben muttered something to the guards as I approached. Their eyes settled on me before they spoke.

President Clarke would like to speak to the both of you.

I looked up at Ben in surprise. Connor had reported the both of us again undoubtedly.

I can take her there.

No, the President stated that we accompany both of you to her office.

Do you really think that's necessary?

An order is an order, Ben.

He rolled his eyes at the guards and nodded for them to begin their duties, jaw tensed. With a guard next to each of us, we began our journey back up to the President's office.

Ben walked straight into her office, not waiting on the guards to knock. Margot seemed only slightly surprised by Ben's abrupt arrival. I followed him into the office, the guards closing the door behind the both of us.

Do you really think guards were necessary, Margot?

Ben, I'm disappointed in you. I hear that you bloodied one of your peers in front of a room full of recruits. That is very unprofessional. Do you realize that reflects on the entire Society when the leader of the guards behaves savagely?

You know Connor is a moron. I don't know why you've been listening to him. He's been a problem for a long time.

Regardless, he tells the truth. His blood could not lie nor could your little friend's presence in your apartment. Really, Ben, what has come over you?

Yes, I shouldn't have lost control today or let Darcy break curfew. I will take full blame for that. But it is none of your concern who I spend my time with.

That is enough, Ben. We will talk later about your behavior. However, I will not let you take the blame for Darcy. She is the one who disobeyed rules.

Ben was about to protest when the President raised her hand to stop him.

I'm sorry, Ben. It is not your choice.

She was leaning on the front of her desk, arms crossed. Turning her attention to me, she looked around Ben and gestured for me to come closer. Her bony finger reminded me of a witch's finger, pale and bony.

Darcy, I have been thinking for the last couple days about how I would like to punish you. Ben came to me after our first conversation and made me rethink my entire perspective.

I looked at Ben, but he wouldn't meet eye contact. He focused out the window at the desert horizon, standing at attention as a soldier before his commanding officer.

Do not look at him. He cannot save you from your punishment. You have created quite a disturbance since you arrived here. So, I have decided to assign you to the field.

This statement shocked Ben out of his silence. He jolted upright and looked at his aunt in disbelief.

You can't possibly be serious! Recruits are sent out after four months of training. She's only been here a little over two months!

Her test scores are high. I believe she will complete the mission I have in mind satisfactorily.

No, it's a suicide mission. She's only halfway through the required training. There must be another punishment.

Enough!

Margot jolted herself with the force she used in her command. She stood up, straightening her blazer and looked at Ben. He had become extremely stoic, void of any emotion.

It is already done. Her train leaves tonight. Darcy, you will be supplied with clothes on location so you will not have to pack. Guards will arrive at your door at six-thirty sharp. You may leave. Ben, stay.

She stood, staring at me with an icy dismissiveness. I couldn't help but think this would be the last time I saw Ben. The closest I'd ever be to him forever. He still stood at attention in front of his aunt, stiff as a board.

I took one last glance at him, remembering the way his hair curled around his temples, the cut of his jaw, the softness in his lips. Then, I crossed the room to the door. Upon opening it, I found the guards prepared to take me back to my apartment.

No, this isn't fair! They can't do this to you. You haven't even been through the entire training!

Kate was infuriated by the news of my premature deployment into the field. She had been protesting for the last ten minutes as I sat on the couch, manipulating a throw pillow between my fingers.

When I was returned to my apartment by the guards, Kate had been sitting in the kitchen waiting for my return. The last time she saw me, I was being taken away by the guards with Ben. After

185

a horde of questions, I explained to her what had happened, starting with Connor and ending with Margot and Ben.

This is all Connor's fault. If he weren't a snitch, none of this would have happened. You guys have been involved for weeks and nothing has happened until he opened his big mouth. I ought to punch his teeth out.

Obviously, hitting him only does more damage. As long as he's whispering in the President's ear, there's nothing we can do. She made it quite obvious she is in control.

And what about the plan? It's over now? We can't do it without you and you're never coming back. I have less than two months left before I'm deployed. The same for the rest of them: Sam and Hannah. Brendan will be the only one staying here.

I sat in defeat, wishing I had more time. More time to finish the plan. More time with Kate and Noah, with my friends I'd made here at the facility. And I hated myself for even thinking it, but I wanted more time with Ben. Before I found out who he was, before I hated myself for loving him.

No, I'll find you all again. Maybe we could do more outside of the facility than in it. We have to wait for the right moment. You'll know when it's time.

There was serious doubt reflecting in her eyes. Tears began to well up in the corners, running down her cheeks.

I might never see you again, Darcy. They're sending you out too early. It's careless of them and dangerous for you.

I'll be fine, Kate. But I will miss you.

She smiled past the tears and threw her arms around my neck. I could feel her warm breath as she mumbled in my ear.

I'm so sorry I didn't tell you about Ben.

It's okay, Kate. I know you didn't want me to get hurt.

Squeezing me tight, she let go and looked down at my neck.

Where'd that come from?

I reached up to feel my neck before realizing I still had on the necklace Ben had given me. So much had been going on, I had forgotten it was there in my absentmindedness.

Oh, it belonged to Ben's mother. I guess I don't need to take this with me. Will you give it back to him? Or have Noah give it back?

No, Darcy. Keep it.

No, I don't feel right taking it with me.

Reaching behind my neck to unclasp it, I watched as Kate wiped the tears from her eyes. She hesitantly took it from me, looking down at the necklace in disappointment.

Give it to him whenever you see him next. I don't want him thinking I took off with it.

I've got a feeling he would want you to. Darcy...

I could tell that she wanted to talk about Ben and his innocence. The emptiness in my chest was enough for me. There was no way that I wanted to talk about it again.

Well, I'm going to go take a nap. There's no point in me going to afternoon classes now. I'll see you after you get back.

She clasped her mouth shut, aware that I cut her off on purpose. Nodding her head, she kept her eyes on the necklace in her hands as I got up from the couch and retreated to my bedroom.

It was only behind my closed door that I lost control. The absence of my mother and Ben and the fear of the unknown mission I was being sent on was all too much. I collapsed on the bed, sobbing uncontrollably until I fell asleep, dreaming of blood, trains, and green eyes.

XV.

TUNNEL VISION

As scheduled, the guards showed up at my door at six-thirty sharp. Waking up from a nap, I showered and dressed in jeans and a jacket. When Kate had returned from her classes, she had Noah with her. He hugged me around my shoulders, encouraging me to be safe and think through every choice.

Moving out from between us, I saw Kate waiting for her hug, small and vulnerable. She attempted to grin but couldn't hide the sadness of my departure.

I walked toward her, opening my arms and wrapping them around her neck. Whispering in her ear, I felt her stiffen as she listened.

I'll miss you. You're my best friend, you know that?

She nodded her head against my shoulder, sniffling.

Don't forget about us.

Although it seemed sentimental, the look in Kate's eyes as she pulled back held more meaning. She didn't want me to forget about the plan. Somehow, she wanted me to figure out how to continue with the plan even after I had left the confines of the facility.

The guard's knock at the door interrupted our goodbyes. Taking a deep breath, I opened the door and stepped out into the hallway. Looking back at Kate with Noah's arm around her shoulder, I nodded in agreement of her statement. I wouldn't forget them. Until the day I died, I would never forget them or my plan. They were forever engrained into my soul, into who I was.

The guards guided me to the elevators, only this time they stopped on the second level. My heart beat in my throat as the doors opened, knowing how close I was to Ben. There was a chance that he was on the other side of those doors.

However, the air was far too cold as Margot stepped into the elevators through the now open doors. She barely noticed my existence as she pressed an unmarked button on the elevator wall, scanning her card against the red light that flashed beside it.

The elevator started its descent once again. However, when we reached ground level, we continued moving. Thinking about the blueprints Sam showed me, I realized that the tunnels were right below the recruits' flats. Literally an elevator ride down.

When the metal doors opened, there was a white hallway lit in fluorescent lighting. It had stone walls painted white with gray concrete floors, making it look like something out of a horror movie. I half expected the lights to flicker. The air was much cooler than the rest of the facility, a draft passing through the hall.

Margot began walking down the hallway, heading toward a set of double doors at the end of the corridor. She scanned her card once again before the doors unlocked loudly and opened slowly. The guards guided me through the opening, allowing me to see the tunnel to which it led.

The mine through the earth was large, housing a subway-like train in its mouth. With a loud screech, the doors shut behind me and loudly locked themselves. Margot stood by the doors of the train with another guard, one I had never seen before.

He was a middle-aged man with graying hair that he kept short on the sides and softly feathered on the top. Together, they spoke in private as I stood next to the guards a good distance away. Her rigidity didn't seem to bother the man as he listened intently to her orders. Suddenly, Margot turned away from the guard and walked toward me, gesturing for the guards to give us privacy.

It is usually a proud occasion when a recruit is sent on their first mission. However, with you, it is a relief. You have caused me trouble since the day you arrived here. Your attitude toward authority is despicable as well as your relationship with my nephew. I think this separation will be best for the both of you.

I glared at her, the bitter taste of hatred in my mouth. When I had challenged her to take more than I had already lost, she succeeded. With so much unknown about where she was sending me, it was better to accept her consequences as is and not worsen the situation.

Well, it seems it only took you getting sent away to shut your mouth. Richard will brief you on the train ride to the next station on your mission. Good luck, Darcy.

I didn't know if it was only in my head or if her goodbye seemed cynical. She turned and gestured for me to approach Richard who stood waiting next to the train. Reaching his side, he nodded to her and she walked back toward the secured doors. His dark brown eyes turned to me and he put his hand out for me to shake.

Richard Ashton. Nice to meet you, Darcy.

Surprised by his pleasant demeanor, I hesitated only for a split second before nodding politely to him. The doors of the train slid open, allowing me to see several benches along its interior walls. He motioned for me to step onto the train.

If you want to have a seat, it's about a thirty-minute ride until we reach the station that ends this hidden tunnel. During that time, I will be briefing you on your assignment.

Sitting down parallel to me in the small area, he maintained eye contact and began his summary.

You have been assigned to the Chicago area. There, you will act as a Guest Relations Manager at a very renowned hotel. Many politicians and public figures use this hotel for their stays and conferences. Throughout your stay there, you will receive several missions, small at first and then growing in significance.

How long will I be there?

There is no set time. The Society observes countless events and situations in the world before deciding when to relocate a recruit. Once the job is done and there is no need at this location, you will be moved as necessary.

I don't have any experience as a hotel manager.

They have taken care of that. Your resume is here in this folder. Study and memorize this. You will have a new alias while you're in the field. The President assures me that you have received enough training in hospitality that you will perform satisfactorily.

So, I'm going to use another name?

Yes, Rebecca Marsh, born in a small town in Indiana. You moved to Chicago for your career, finding this position most recently. They are expecting you to begin on Monday. Today is Saturday. You will be in your new living quarters by Sunday.

How exactly did I get the job without a single interview?

Let's just say that the Influencers have connections just about everywhere in the world. As for your job duties, they are listed there in the folder.

I looked down at the folder he had passed me. Opening it, I found a biography of my alias, resume, and job description near the front of the paperwork. The paper listed several tasks including: manage needs of VIP guests, greet and direct visitors, resolve issues, and make sure guest stay is perfect.

Behind that page, a satellite image showed the hotel between countless other buildings close to Lake Michigan. I had never been to Chicago, recounting the stories I heard of its harsh winters and busy streets.

Your apartment is already stocked with the essentials: food, clothes, toiletries. Feel free to ask any questions before we reach the next station.

Are you coming with me to Chicago?

I will make the journey with you to ensure seamless entry into your outside environment and then return to my station.

Then, why do I have to ask my questions before that?

Well, the Society doesn't want anyone knowing where the entrance to the tunnel is so you will be given medication to sleep while we transport you.

Of course.

It's only a mild sedative. You'll just take a quick nap and then wake up before our flight.

I'm guessing it's the same stuff I got knocked out with when I was brought here.

Let's just say that it will not be your first unconscious ride in this train.

I rolled my eyes and returned my gaze to him. He seemed amused at my hatred of the sedative.

Well, make sure to study everything in the folder. We have a little bit of time still yet.

Over the next thirty minutes, I memorized my new identity and duties. I couldn't help but think of what the Society had planned for me. Brendan had seen too many malevolent files in their system for this to be a role merely ensuring the comfort of hotel guests. There had to be more.

Images of Ben flashed into my mind throughout the train ride. I remembered the night that we had spent together in his apartment. We lay there under the covers together in his bed. I looked into his green eyes, kissing his mouth softly.

His hands ran down my back, as he lay there studying my face. The smell of his cologne, his soap filled my nostrils.

Darcy, I don't ever want to let you go.

Drawing closer to his body, I kissed him deeply before pulling back to look into his eyes.

Then, don't.

The sound of the train brought me out of my daydream. Shaking my head, I focused on the mission that lay ahead of me. I couldn't let thoughts of him ruin my concentration. From now on, I had to see only the mission ahead and forget about everything else, even Ben.

I felt hands on my back as I bent forward, heaving into a bag in front of me. Richard supported me as I emptied bile from my stomach. Sitting back, I looked over at him unamused.

In the back of a black sedan, Richard sat on the other end of the seat. He removed his hands from my back and placed them in his lap.

You guys really have to stop drugging me.

I'm sorry. That should be the last time. They are very serious about keeping certain information secret. If you are okay to move, we don't want to miss our flight.

I looked out the window and found that we were in the departure's lane of an airport. Nodding in readiness, Richard exited the sedan and circled the back of the car to help me out.

It was odd feeling the outside air. For two months, I had not been outside of the air conditioning that the facility provided. Breathing in the fresh air, I smelled sunshine, trees, and rain. The airport was obviously a distance from the facility as I saw greenery around the airport.

Richard placed his hand on my shoulder and gestured toward the entrance of the airport. He handed me my plane ticket and picture ID, separating his paperwork from mine.

I'm surprised they let us use the same airplanes as civilians and not use their own private jet.

You're a part of the real world now, Darcy. You have to blend in. And normal people do not have private jets whisk them around the country.

We made our way to the security check, weaving in and out of crowds of people. Having reached the group of waiting people,

I tensed at the thought of passing the fake identification card to the security guard. The line to the desk moved quickly, my heartrate increasing the closer Richard and I got. He leaned down, mumbling quietly into my ear.

You're fine. I assure you the Society is not sloppy when it comes to faking identifications. There's no way you will be detained. Trust me, I've done this a hundred times.

Has anyone ever been caught?

Only one but he's no longer with us.

The shock on my face was evident, my jaw dropping immediately. I heard a low rumble coming from Richard as he chuckled at my reaction.

It was a joke, Darcy.

Not a funny one.

He looked at me out of the corner of his eye, still grinning mischievously.

You're going to have to learn to relax under pressure. This is nothing compared to missions the Society will assign to you.

His reassurance had now become reminder of the hard reality I was being forced to accept. I felt extremely unprepared as he made me aware of the level of stress I felt at my first and probably smallest task.

There were only three people in front of us now, the guard signing their boarding passes one by one. Richard took a step forward as the security guard called for the next person. He

197

handed him his identification and boarding pass then was guided toward the metal detectors.

Suddenly, the guard looked at me, motioning for me to approach. I swallowed the rock in my throat, stepped forward, and handed him my paperwork. He looked between me and the ID card then signed my boarding pass.

I accepted it back and joined Richard in line for the metal detectors. He grinned at me as I approached him, clearly amused by the relief on my face.

I told you there was nothing to worry about.

Forgive me if I don't have faith in them.

Together we took our shoes off and emptied our pockets. Richard allowed me to pass through the metal detectors before him this time, waiting behind while they checked me. After the metal detectors, we found our gate and boarded the plane headed to O'Hare Airport.

Waiting for the plane to take off after boarding, Richard and I sat in our seats next to one another. He sat reading a magazine he had pulled from behind the seat. Several passengers were still placing their luggage in the overhead compartments.

So, what made you want to choose this... career?

I was a good friend of the people who created the group. The Lewis's. Nice couple. Too bad what happened to them.

I tensed hearing him refer to Ben's parents. He had known them when they first created the Society, when it was still benevolent.

You knew the founders?

Oh, yeah. Me and Charles were friends in school. He was always a very kind man, extremely intelligent. After high school, I joined the military. Years later, Charles and his wife, Olivia, found me. They offered me a job and I've never looked back since.

What about their son? Did you know him?

Uh, yeah, I remember their son, Ben. Sweet kid. Always shook my hand when he saw me.

I couldn't help but smile. Ben, before the death of his parents and the harsh raising by his aunt. Sweet Ben.

What would you want to do if you weren't in the Society?

Ben's green eyes met mine from the other pillow. We lay in bed, not tired enough to sleep. There was no moonlight to illuminate my bedroom that night, the room around us quite dark. After a while, our eyes had adjusted so that we could see one another. He was silent as he gave serious thought to my question.

I don't know. I would want to help people though. I've always thought of going back to the South Sudan region that my parents helped before they passed.

You would want to go back to where your parents were killed?

I don't want to think about it like that. It's something they were passionate about and I want to finish their work.

Wow. That's beautiful.

And you? What did you have planned before coming here?

Well, I was working in an office trying to afford college. I was thinking about going into nursing. To help the people when they're sick like my mom. Make it easier on them and their families.

He was quiet, digesting the information. Moving closer to me, he brushed his hand against my cheek.

Since I met you, I've thought a lot about what life would be like outside of these walls. A life we could build together.

Oh, and what would that involve?

His hands found mine, wrapping them in his gentle warmth. The focus in his eyes told me he was remembering his past.

Well, there was this cabin that only my parents and I knew about, not even any of our family. We would go there to get away. I imagined us there, away from the world, just the two of us.

Is it still there?

I have no idea. After they passed, I kept its existence to myself. I felt like if I shared it with anyone, I was giving a part of my parents away. It was our secret hideout.

And now you're telling me. Not so secret anymore, Benjamin.

Well, that makes it our secret, doesn't it?

A gleam ran across his eyes before he pressed his lips against mine. His warmth overwhelmed me and made my eyes heavy. I buried my head against his chest and drifted off, dreaming of our secret cabin in the woods.

Darcy? Darcy.

Quickly, I escaped from my daydream as Richard attempted to get my attention. His face showed confusion at my sudden inattention.

Huh?

I said did you know him? He's a guard at the facility.

Green eyes, dark hair that curled on the ends, soft lips, the ripple of muscle in his abdomen, his presence hovering over me.

Yeah, I met him.

Richard didn't seem to believe my statement. He studied my face for more information before finally giving up and going back to his magazine. The plane started moving suddenly and the pilot announced the weather and estimated time of arrival in Chicago.

I rested my head on the back of my seat, allowing my eyes to close. No matter how hard I tried to focus on the mission ahead, my mind somehow would always lead back to Ben. My heart, my mind, my soul. They would always lead back to him.

XVI.

CITY BY THE LAKE

Richard and I exited the plane down the long, enclosed hallway. Having left the facility in the evening, both the train and plane ride pushed our arrival time to early morning. I had never been to O'Hare or Chicago, so I was surprised by the amount of people active and businesses still open at that time.

Grabbing a taxi outside of the airport, Richard told the cab driver our destination and sat back in his seat. He looked as tired as I felt. During the plane ride, we had both slept for a short period of time.

The taxi weaved between traffic through the city. Outside of the window, the sky was still black which only illuminated the city lights and towering buildings. Window displays presented expensive jewelry and designer clothing.

After twenty minutes of driving through traffic, the taxi stopped in front of a brick apartment building. Richard handed the cab driver money before opening his door and getting out of the car. I reached for the handle and found Richard on the other side of the door, extending his hand to help me step up on the street curb.

He was constantly a gentleman, opening doors and offering help. Every kind act only made me realize how many good people worked for the Society. Kate, Noah, Richard. They were all kind, good-hearted people who worked for an unknowingly malevolent cult.

Richard and I entered the lobby of the apartment building, heading toward the elevators on the right side of the room. The lobby was pleasant, simple in design and clean. Furniture filled the middle of the room, modern with sharp lines.

The elevator interrupted my observation of the room as its bell rang letting us know it had arrived. Richard stepped forward, placing his hand over the door and pressing the button for the third floor.

He allowed me to exit the doors first before following behind me, gesturing for me to turn left. The sound of keys jingling rang through the air as Richard unlocked the apartment door.

He entered the apartment, finding the light switch before turning to face me.

This will be your new apartment. One bedroom, one bathroom. It's got a small living room and kitchen that will suit you perfectly. Come on, I'll show you around.

The short hallway coming from the entrance opened to the living room. Richard was right when he said small. It held enough room for one long couch and a tv stand.

Having an open concept, the living room and kitchen were one room. The kitchen stood behind the couch with two stools next to its small island. There were a handful of cabinets surrounding the sink and refrigerator, crowned with marble countertops.

A small hallway behind the kitchen led to the bedroom and attached bathroom. The bedroom was roomier than the rest of the apartment, housing a queen bed, dresser, and small walk-in closet. Margot hadn't lied when she said they would supply my clothes. The entire closet was filled with both business and casual attire.

Inside the bathroom, I found a stand-in shower with glass doors, a toilet, and small vanity. Though the apartment was obviously created for one person, it was clean and well designed.

However, I couldn't help but think how odd it would be not sharing it with anyone else. I had grown accustomed to living in the flat with Kate and most of the time, Noah and Ben. Looking at the bed, my chest ached with emptiness. I would be sleeping alone now, too.

Not as big as the flat back at the facility but I hope you still find it generous.

Yes, it's nice.

He cleared his throat and leaned on the doorframe of the bedroom, looking down at the floor.

It's late and you need your rest before you start work Monday. And technically...

Raising his wrist to look at his watch, he met eye contact with me.

You start work tomorrow. Get some sleep. I'll be on the couch.

I nodded my head and watched as he closed the door behind him. Immediately, I collapsed on the bed, clothes and all. Sleep consumed me instantly.

Sunlight coming through the window in the bedroom woke me from my sleep. Slowly, I sat up and looked around at my surroundings. I had forgotten where I was, waking from my dreams of being back at the facility.

I could hear noise coming from outside of my bedroom door. The clanging of pots and pans. Sliding off the bed, I walked into the hallway and down toward the kitchen.

When I rounded the corner, I found Richard standing over the stovetop built into the kitchen island. Its glass top cooking surface had caused it to go unnoticed earlier that morning. He looked up at the sound of my approach, grinning in welcome.

Good morning. I was hungry and thought you might like eggs, too.

From the skillet in his hands, he slid two sunny-side-up eggs onto a plate with toast and handed it to me. The smell of eggs wafted to my nose and caused my empty stomach to growl. I took the plate gladly and sat down on one of the stools at the island.

Richard continued to make his breakfast, cracking two eggs into the same skillet. He hummed as he moved around the kitchen, grabbing a carton of orange juice out of the fridge and a glass out of one of the cabinets.

Today, I will show you where you will be working and give you a tour of the neighborhood. Groceries will be delivered every Sunday morning, so you won't have to worry about going shopping. A maid will come in throughout the week while you work to tidy up the place and take away your dirty laundry.

And I thought I was supposed to act normal now.

You will. Many people who work in the city have groceries delivered or pay a maid to clean their house.

Having poured each of us a glass of juice and grabbing his eggs off the stove, he sat on the stool next to me and ate his breakfast. The entire apartment was silent except for the clinking of our silverware on the dishes.

Having finished his eggs, Richard gulped the rest of his orange juice down and placed his plate in the sink.

If you don't mind, I'm going to clean up in the bathroom while you finish your breakfast.

Nodding my approval, I looked down at my half-eaten eggs and toast. The yolk streaked yellow across the plate as it ran out of the eggs and into the corners of the toast. I couldn't help but remember the first meal Kate had made for me upon arriving at the flat on my first day there. She had made scrambled eggs and toast.

For wanting so much to escape the confinement of the facility, I sure missed being there. I missed all the friends that I had made while there. Friends that I might never see again. In a way, I was hidden from all the dangers of the world. Out of the facility, I felt vulnerable, unprotected.

The realization depleted my appetite, scraping the leftover eggs into the trashcan and placing the plate on top of Richard's in the sink. I walked over to the window by the couch and looked out at the view. The street below was filled with pedestrians ranging from mothers with their children to businessmen in suits.

Across the street were shorter buildings than the one in which I stood, small shops. A flower shop, a deli, a pawn shop. Overhead, the sky was bright blue without a single cloud. Richard came from the back of the apartment, looking refreshed.

Thank you very much. Now, if you will go get ready, we will be on our way.

The streets were busy, filled with cars, buses, and taxi cabs, as we made our way to the hotel where I would be employed. Breathing in the beauty of the day, I could smell the water from Lake Michigan. The lake sat only a few blocks from the hotel, providing a cool breeze between the buildings.

Looking up at the countless stories of the hotel building, I noticed the air of sophistication that it held. Even the doors to the lobby looked like they cost a fortune. Inside the window, I could see several individuals in suits, conversing over a cup of coffee in the lounge area.

Richard explained to me that the hotel was prestigious and well-known by politicians, world leaders, celebrities, and other affluent individuals.

He continued to walk down the street until we reached the crosswalk. After we had reached the other side of the street, Richard made his way to a small coffee shop directly across from the hotel. The aroma of freshly ground coffee beans filled the air outside of the store windows.

Let's sit down and talk a moment. Would you like a cup of coffee?

Yes, please.

The lack of sleep from the night before still lingered even as we walked around the city. Richard went up to the counter and ordered our drinks. Meanwhile, I found a small booth close to the window that would provide privacy from the other coffee house customers.

After a moment, he made his way back with two paper cups, handing me one and keeping one for himself. Sitting across from me in the booth, Richard sipped his cup of coffee. I grabbed the sugar that was provided on the table and added it to my cup, just enough to tame the bitterness of the drink.

The hot sweetness of the coffee was comforting as I sipped it, listening to Richard. It warmed me from the inside out in the harsh air-conditioning of the café.

Now, you should arrive tomorrow morning at nine 'o'clock. You are to find a Mr. Johnson. He is the Vice President of Guest Relations for the hotel who will provide you with the information you will need: location of your office, overview of your duties, and any paperwork that might need completed.

He looked out the window to the hotel as he explained further.

You will have small missions for the first couple weeks of being at your position. Nothing that will throw up any flags to others. Here is your phone. This is how the Society communicates with you. Keep it with you at all times.

Out of his pocket, he pulled a black phone and set it on the table in front of me. I picked it up and rolled it between my two hands.

I assume there's a tracking device in this, too?

Yes. If it goes out of range of the device implanted under your skin, then it will shut down and factory reset to delete all evidence of communication with the Society. It's a safeguard.

Yeah, I bet.

Richard looked at me out of the corner of his eye, puzzled by my sarcastic comment. I looked out the window and sipped my coffee. I was tempted to share with him my discoveries about the Society but didn't know the extent of his loyalty.

The lump in my throat only grew as the urge to tell him everything surfaced.

Richard, how much do you really know about the missions the Society sends the recruits to complete?

Not much. They are very careful about letting any one person know too much about their activities. I am only told that small missions are given to prove the recruit's ability before the larger missions are assigned.

I tried my best to read his face as I continued to question him. For some reason, I felt like I could trust Richard. He had been kind and respectful the entire time I knew him. His connection to Ben's parents only made it more complicated to understand where his loyalty was placed: in the benevolent Society that Ben's parents created or in the one that existed now.

Yet, as I sat there with him in the coffee shop, I couldn't shake the feeling that I should tell him. I tiptoed onto the subject, aware of any signals to stop.

Would you believe me if I told you the Society wasn't what it was created to be?

It's normal for a group to evolve as it operates. If not, it would not succeed in the ever-changing world.

No, not just improving and adapting… but changing, changing its entire reason for existing.

What are you talking about, Darcy? There's no way that's possible.

How could you be so sure?

Richard's mouth opened to answer the question, but he found himself speechless. He shook his head, looking down at the table and then out the window. His eyes followed people as they passed the coffee shop.

I'm not sure. But do you know what that would mean? I would've been helping this whole time, wasting my life on a career that didn't make a difference in the world. It's not something that you should just throw around casually, Darcy.

I know.

There's a lot of people out there that are under the assumption that they're helping the world by being a part of this Society. All the recruits that train thinking they are changing society for the better.

But there's a lot more people that are going to get hurt, innocent people.

How do you know this. Darcy?

I can't say. I shouldn't have even put you in danger like this. If they find out…

Darcy, if you're right in your suspicions, you have to understand that you can't win. They have people everywhere, eyes and ears everywhere. Trust me.

I shook my head, looking around at the customers in the coffee house. There was no way of knowing who was listening or watching us. I shouldn't have told him. I endangered his safety.

Richard leaned forward and met eye contact with me, speaking very low.

Darcy, I had my suspicions before. I started to catch on when the horrible events taking place in the world were the locations of recruits I had transported. But you've got to let it go. There is no escape, no way to defeat them. Even members thousands of miles away are afraid to go rogue. They know they'd be surrounded in an instant.

Thoughts of the plans I had made with Kate, Brendan, and the other recruits ran through my mind. But I had to be careful who knew about the plan. Too many people would only risk it.

He watched me carefully as I nodded in what he thought was surrender. I had to make him think that I had given up.

Darcy, just promise me that you'll be careful. Do as they say and watch your back.

I will.

The possibilities of what I just agreed to were endless. I had no idea what missions I would be assigned. My chest felt heavy as I looked across the table at Richard, promising to do anything the Society told me to do.

After we finished our coffees, Richard took me back to my apartment and wished me luck. He was due to fly back to the facility in a couple hours. I could see the concern for me in his eyes as he shook my hand at the door.

Good luck, Darcy. If we never see each other again, I want you to know that it was real pleasure meeting you.

You too, Richard. Thanks for everything.

The door shut behind him, leaving me alone in my new apartment. I looked around the living room, feeling more tired than I had that morning. But the bed provided no temptation. I knew that I would feel even lonelier there. The other side of the bed would only remind me of how empty it was, how empty it had been the last days, how empty it would always be.

I collapsed onto the couch and fell asleep. When I woke up, it was night. Rolling over on the couch, I looked out the window at the moon, a silver sliver in the sky.

I couldn't help but wonder if Ben had looked at that same moon that night. If he had remembered the night of our first kiss in front of the desert moon. The warmth of him under my hands, the softness of his kiss. Every tiny detail of him ran through my head, through every fiber of my being.

The grief that rested heavy on my chest was too much to take. I couldn't fight it anymore, couldn't stop myself from thinking about him. I laid on my side, looking at the moon until I surrendered to the temporary relief that dreams of Ben provided.

XVII.

DAILY GRIND

The alarm on my phone sounded, waking me from the couch. I jumped up and ran to the bedroom, throwing open the closet door. Rummaging through the business attire that I was provided, I found a blouse and pencil skirt to wear and threw it on the bed.

I quickly jumped into the shower and washed away the past couple days of travel and stress. Nervous for the day ahead of me, I reviewed over and over again what I had learned at the facility: etiquette, language, business. Drying off, I went to the vanity and found a blow dryer, makeup, and a hair straightener.

After I had gotten ready, I looked in the mirror over the bathroom sink and analyzed my work. The pencil skirt and blouse fit me perfectly with high heels to match and my straight hair and neutral shades of makeup provided a sense of sophistication and maturity that I believed would fit my role.

I had enough time after getting dressed to make a cup of coffee, find a travel mug, and run out the door. As I walked briskly to the front door of the hotel, I almost didn't recognize the businesswoman looking back at me in the reflection of the windows.

I approached the front desk, introducing myself as Rebecca Marsh, and asked for Mr. Johnson. They directed me to walk down a hallway to the left and find the door with his name on it.

A firm knock on his door provoked a man to call out, giving me permission to enter. Behind the desk, a man, most likely in his sixties looked up from his paperwork. His hair was nearly all gray and he wore a white shirt with a gray tie and pants. As soon as he saw me, he stood up and reached his hand across the desk in welcome.

You must be Rebecca Marsh. Pleased to make your acquaintance.

Pleased to meet you, Mr. Johnson.

Well, let me show you to your office. It's just down the hallway here to the right.

He extended his hand so that I would walk into the hallway first and then followed me out. Turning to the right, he started down the hallway. A few doors down from his office was a door labeled Rebecca Marsh, Guest Relations Manager.

How do you like your door? We had your name tag made last week.

Very nice, sir.

Smiling, he opened the door to my office and flipped the light switch on the wall beside the entrance. The room was sizable for an unshared office, housing a desk, a decorative table, and a small couch.

Wow, this is very generous. Thank you, sir.

Well, we like to treat our employees very well here. Unhappy employees make for unhappy customers. Now, I'd like to go over some of the upcoming events here at the hotel and what we expect from you.

Okay, that would be great.

First, there is a national championship for robotics here in the city this week. We have guests from that event booked throughout the hotel. Part of their tournament is being held in our large conference center. You will be expected to make sure they have everything they need and that the guests are happy.

Absolutely.

Then, we have some Congressmen visiting the city over the span of the next couple weeks. You will also be in charge of managing their needs and resolving any issues that may arise with their stay here.

It would be an honor.

Lastly, three weeks from now, there will be an extremely prestigious peace conference held in our conference center. It will involve global peace leaders and countless members of various companies here in the city as well as the public. You are to organize, direct, and oversee every aspect of their stay here and their event.

Understood.

We are looking forward to you joining our team here, Ms. Marsh. With your experience, I believe you're going to make a great fit.

My chest tightened as he mentioned the resume the Society had built for me to get this job. Quickly, I went over the memorized history in my head in case he had questions.

However, he had no inquiries and merely started for the door, turning around once he had nearly reached the exit.

Oh, I have only a couple items of paperwork for you to sign before you are free to start your work. Let me go grab them. I'll be right back.

After he left, I surveyed my new office, sitting in the desk chair and rearranging a few items on the desk. So far, my office was lovely, and Mr. Johnson was extremely professional and welcoming. Yet, it was not the hotel that made me nearly as nervous as the missions I would be sent by the Society to complete.

For the first few days of work, this worry weighed heavily on my shoulders. I was constantly checking my phone in moments of privacy, making sure the Society had not tried to contact me.

However, there was no communication from the Society. I used the time to get to know the staff at the hotel and grow confident in my ability to assist customers. Issues were resolved in a timely manner and the staff was organized in their duties to ensure a smooth operation.

In all honesty, I preferred working rather than being alone in my apartment. At work, there were people to converse with and keep me company.

Then, on the fourth day of my employment, I received a message from the Society on my phone. It was early enough in the morning that I had not yet arrived at work. The phone buzzed and revealed the message: AN ENVELOPE WILL BE ON YOUR DESK, DO NOT OPEN. DELIVER TO ROOM 2242 AT 11AM SHARP.

Sure enough, there was a manila envelope left on my desk whenever I unlocked my office door that morning. How and when the envelope was placed in my locked office, I had no idea. Leave it to the Society to make locks look useless.

Since I began work at nine in the morning, I still had two hours to kill before the envelope had to be delivered. I headed out to the front desk to receive a summary of the scheduled visitors for that day. The rest of the morning went on like usual, greeting and directing visitors and managing staff on any problems that customers may have had.

Finally, I looked at my watch and saw that I had ten minutes before delivery was scheduled. I made my way back to my office, grabbed the manila envelope, and headed for the elevators.

The twenty-second floor took some time to reach on the elevator, building the anticipation of the assignment. I had no idea who I was delivering the envelope to or what it contained. Although I had the resources to obtain the guest's identity, a small amount of fear discouraged my search.

Four minutes remained as I walked down the hall, searching for the room 2242. Finally, I reached the door, waiting until the time on my phone changed to 11AM before knocking on the door.

I could hear feet shuffling behind the door and feel someone's gaze through the peephole. Then, the door cracked open. The room was dark, and I couldn't see a face in the black gap between the door and its frame.

A hand reached out to take the envelope and then the door immediately shut. After a moment's hesitation, I walked away from the door briskly. Although the sinister hand had shaken my nerves, I had just successfully completed my first mission.

For the next couple weeks, small tasks were given to me similar to the first: delivering envelopes, making sure certain visitors got certain rooms or reservations, or messaging the Society on when certain guests arrived or checked out.

I was starting to become confident in my ability to complete missions. In fact, the overwhelming worry I had felt with assignments before now became adrenaline that fueled my abilities.

In the first week of the deployment, I was incredibly lonely at night. No matter if I was in the living room, kitchen, or bedroom, I found myself turning to tell Noah about a joke or tell Kate about my day. It felt odd not following the normal routine of the Society with their morning lessons, lunch break, and afternoon sessions every day of the week.

The nights were the hardest. For the last month, Ben had either been in the same room or in the bed next to me. The blankets felt cold devoid of the warmth he provided. For the first week, I would turn over in my sleep and search for him. When I didn't find him, my eyes would open, and reality would settle heavy into my chest.

During the following two weeks, I became acquainted with several people at work. Mr. Johnson proved to be a great companion during lunches, dropping by several times to share our lunch break together. He would show me pictures of his children and grandchildren, glowing in pride and adoration of them.

There were a couple of women behind the front desk who offered to take me out for dinner after work from time to time. Though I accepted their offer, I couldn't help but wish Kate were there.

As I began to memorize names and faces, the job became easier. No longer was I a stranger in an unknown environment but a person who everyone knew and asked questions. Three weeks following my arrival, I felt comfortable with my surroundings and my job.

However, my greatest hurdle at the job was still to come. Mr. Johnson had warned me of the peace conference to be held at the hotel, bringing with it high-status politicians, celebrities, and other public figures. Every detail had to be planned and executed perfectly.

This event would be the test of my abilities. Up until now, every task seemed miniscule. Not only did the event have to be seamless, but also the public figures' stay at the hotel. It was up to me to manage and organize the staff to meet this goal.

As the time approached for the event, I found myself making notes while at my apartment during the night, reminding myself of tasks to be completed and in what order. The event consumed me. Yet, the fact that it was a peace conference and I was working for a violent Society lingered in the back of my mind constantly.

It was that same fact that drove me to make sure every detail of the event and the guests' stay was perfect, almost too perfect to ruin without public notice.

Catering, employee assignments, transportation, reservations, and scheduling were completed, and the event was only a day away. The Society had grown eerily quiet this week, not sending any assignment thus far.

The hotel buzzed with excitement, inviting visitors and setting up the conference center. I walked down the hallway toward the enormous room.

Entering through the double doors, I looked around at all the work that had been accomplished. Hundreds of chairs sat facing the stage which sat higher than the audience members to allow for better viewing. Small arrangements of flowers were placed around the room to provide softness and decoration to the monotony of the chairs.

A podium, microphones, and speakers were already set up on stage. As I scanned the room, I found that every item on my list had been accomplished. Looking at my watch, I saw it was already five-o-clock. I headed back toward my office to grab my belongings before leaving for the night.

Walking past Mr. Johnson's office, I noticed he still sat at his desk. As I slowed by his doorway, he looked up from his computer screen over his glasses.

Miss Marsh, I presume everything is in order for the big event tomorrow?

Yes, sir. I believe it's going to be fantastic.

Wonderful. I knew you could do it. I must say you are doing terrific in this position.

Thank you, sir. That means a lot. I was nervous moving to a new city, but I think I've gotten the hang of it.

Well, good. Get a good night's rest. Tomorrow is a big day!

Yes, it is. Have a good night.

Later that night, I had only wished that Mr. Johnson's advice was not easier said than done. Tossing and turning in my bed, I woke constantly from dreams about mishaps during the event.

Near the end of every dream, I would see Margot's face in the audience, looking directly at me and smirking. I couldn't shake the feeling I would hear from them tomorrow and it would be so much more than delivering an envelope.

XVIII.

HARD-KNOCK

On the morning of the event, I was up before the alarm clock went off. Though I made toast with peanut butter and sliced bananas, I could only eat a couple of bites before my nervous stomach refused anymore.

I settled for a cup of coffee as I ran out the door of my apartment, keys in one hand and travel mug in the other. For the special occasion, I had chosen slacks and a blazer over a silk blouse. My heels made hurrying down the sidewalks toward the hotel difficult while also increasing the risk of spilling coffee on my clothes.

The staff were already in action when I arrived in the lobby. The front desk staff greeted and directed guests to where they needed to go, catering was already in full swing back in the kitchen, and Mr. Johnson was conversing to the keynote speakers.

When he noticed my arrival, he gestured for me to wait for him to finish his conversation. With a hand gesture toward the conference center hallway and a smile, Mr. Johnson dismissed himself from the conversation.

Miss Marsh, the speakers have arrived just on time and are waiting for a tour of the hotel and conference center. I told them

you would be with them immediately so hurry and drop your things
off at your office and come right back.

And everything else... it's good?

Working like a well-oiled machine.

He winked at me before I retreated to my office, smiling the entire way. When I returned, I introduced myself to the group of speakers and began the tour. Finally, we reached the conference center which earned several smiles as the speakers filed in through the doorway.

One of the speakers, an ambassador from the Middle East, walked up to me while his colleagues spoke about their queues and seating arrangements on stage.

You have done a wonderful job here. Mr. Johnson tells me all of this was your doing.

Well, I could not have done it without the hard work of my staff. They are the ones who made it possible.

Do not be so modest. Every year that we have held this conference here, it has not been nearly as organized or beautiful as this year's event.

Thank you, sir. That means a lot.

No, thank you. You are making it possible for us to speak to the public, to share the need for peace in the world between every nation, race, and culture. Every small decision and action make a difference in the world. Never forget your impact.

With an appreciative nod, he returned to his colleagues near the front of the stage. After they had finished their discussion, I assigned several employees to show each of the speakers to their rooms.

For the rest of the morning, I answered questions for the staff and prevented any issues from occurring. Although the peace conference started at one in the afternoon, there didn't seem to be enough time in the day. Before I knew it, the morning had passed, and the event was set to begin in the next half hour.

Mr. Johnson was socializing with many of the VIP guests, guiding them to their seats in the conference center. Staff members scurried around, keeping guests happy and the hotel organized and clean.

Eventually, the speakers took their place on the stage and the audience quieted. Mr. Johnson, several employees, and I stood outside of the double doors, watching as the peace conference began.

Suddenly, my heart stopped as I felt the vibrate of the phone in my pocket. I excused myself and walked down the hallway, making my way back to my office. I looked down at my phone when I was sure no one was nearby.

OPEN THE PACKAGE ON YOUR DESK.

Picking up my pace, I turned the corner of the hallway leading to my office. Quickly, I unlocked the door and shut it softly behind me. There, on my desk, sat a small box.

My chest pounded harder and harder as I slowly walked toward my desk. The box could easily be opened with the single flap at the top. In the very bottom of the container sat a small black cube. Carefully, I picked it up to inspect it and found it opened much like a jewelry box.

The beat of my chest was growing louder and louder by the second. Inside of the clasped black box was a single button. Not knowing what it did, I shut the device and looked in the box for more information. Nothing.

Then, my phone vibrated on the desk.

TRIGGER THE DEVICE AT 1:20PM. STAY CLEAR OF THE CONFERENCE CENTER. RETURN TO YOUR APARTMENT IMMEDIATELY.

Stay clear of the conference center when I press the button? It only took half of a second to realize what the Society had planned. They had planted a bomb in the conference center.

Millions of thoughts raced through my head. The other projects Brendan had found in their system, Richard's suspicion, the hundreds of people in the conference center.

I remembered Richard telling me none of the recruits in the field ever went rogue because they would be surrounded immediately. The tracking device would prevent me from destroying the trigger and running away, unless I wanted to cut into my arm. Yet, with so many members, they would likely find me without the chip in my arm.

Then, the countless thoughts ceased and only one rang through my entire being:

Every small decision and action make a difference in the world. Never forget your impact.

Suddenly, I sprang into action. I grabbed the device and used an envelope opener to pry open the back of the small black box. Inside was a tiny motherboard linked to the button. I detached the cords to the button, thereby rendering it useless.

The device fell to the floor, using the heel of my shoe to crush it to pieces. Then, I took off to the conference center. If I could warn everyone, we could evacuate and prevent the bombs from hurting anyone if they were to go off.

My heels were making it difficult to run. Every second counted. Every second could be someone's life that I failed to save. My bare feet pounded against the carpeted floor in the hallway as I flew out of my heels.

Several employees and visitors looked at me like I was insane as I sprinted past them in the hallways. As I turned the corner, I glanced quickly at my watch and found that I only had five minutes until the original detonation time.

Doubts of evacuating that many people in a small amount of time ran across my mind. But I had to try.

My feet couldn't possibly move faster as desperation fueled me. I was rounding the corner of the conference center hallway when I saw Mr. Johnson still standing in the entrance with a few other staff members.

Run! Run! There's a bo---

Confusion ran across their face as they watched me sprint toward them. Then, there was a sudden burst of fire out of the entrance of the conference center. My feet slammed hard against the carpet as the entire building shook under the impact of the explosion.

I could hear screaming from inside the conference center. Mr. Johnson rolled over onto his side, revealing he had several severe burns on the side of his body that faced the door. He appeared stunned as he looked around.

Miss Marsh, what—

Running over to where he lay, his eyes struggled to focus on my face. He was most likely concussed from the impact of the bomb. Smoke had begun pouring into the hallway.

Shh... It's okay. Just sit there. Help will come.

I turned toward the billows of smoke pouring into the hall. My eyes stung as I stood in the entrance, thinking of a way that I could help the people in the blinding smoke. Then, a hand was on my arm. However, it wasn't friendly. The hand squeezed hard enough to sting my skin, pulling me away from the entrance of the conference center.

Looking down through the smoke, I found that Mr. Johnson had lost consciousness, lying stiff on the floor. The other employees in the hallway hadn't moved since the initial blow. Roughly, the hand pulled me over their bodies, forcing me back down the hallway. Once I could see through the smoke, I saw a man in his thirties in front of me with a grasp on my arm.

He must have been with the Society, assigned to remove me. I twisted my arm out of his grasp and stood ready for his reaction. Whirling around, he swung his fist at my face. He was quick but I was ready, fueled by my hatred of the Society and of the murder they had committed today.

Dodging his blow, I placed a punch to his throat as he lunged forward. A choking noise escaped from his lips as his hands flew to grasp his neck. Standing straight up, he approached me once again. His stocky build caused him to be slower, making it easier for me to predict his moves.

Another swing was directed for my ribs, but I blocked it, sweeping my leg across his face in one swift kick. He fell to the ground unconscious from the strike. Making sure he was down for good, I stood and watched him for a moment before heading back toward the screaming in the conference center.

Yet, much to my surprise, there stood behind me a woman in her forties with severe cheekbones and black hair. Before I knew it, she struck me across the face with a hard object in her hand. I fell to the ground, my temple spasming in pain. My vision was blurred as I saw her feet come into view right next to me.

With a prick on my arm, darkness destroyed any chance of further combat.

When I awoke, the metal ceiling of a subway car was above me. I had been haphazardly thrown onto one of the bench seats, my arms and legs hanging over the edge. My stomach was extremely nauseated from the sedative I had been given but I couldn't seem to vomit.

My eyes were still heavy as I struggled to sit up and look around at my surroundings. The window beside me showed that we were underground in the tunnels belonging to the Society. They hadn't just killed me quickly, they were taking me back, back to Margot.

Another wave of nausea washed over me and I bent over, wishing the relief of vomit would come.

What's with you and vomiting every single time you're drugged?

Richard's familiar voice sounded through the subway car. My drowsy eyes searched for him, finding him in the opposite corner of the enclosure. His soft eyes looked burdened.

I swear if you guys drug me one more time...

His deep chuckle traveled over to where I sat, still bent over in agony.

Be careful what you say, Darcy. You are already wanted by the Society. Don't dig your hole any deeper than it already is.

Rich, they bombed a peace conference. There were hundreds of people in there. And I couldn't help them.

I warned you not to rock the boat, Darcy. They're everywhere. You were to do what they told you to do.

I'm not a murderer. I will never let them make me that.

You won't ever get the chance to, Darcy.

What was I supposed to do, just kill hundreds of people and then leave for the next mission?

There was no choice. Now look where you are.

I sat there, feeling utterly defeated as he scolded me. His arms were crossed over his chest like a disappointed father reprimanding his daughter.

As I furrowed my eyebrows in agony over my nausea, pain rippled through the right side of my face. My fingers carefully grazed over my temple where I had been struck, feeling the swelling that had already set in.

Then, it hit me. There should have been a flight between Chicago and here.

Hold on. How did I get here? I've been knocked out since the hotel in Chicago.

Let's just say you finally got your ride in their private jet.

The screams coming from the conference center haunted my thoughts, over and over again. I could still smell smoke on my clothes. Looking down, my blazer was missing, leaving the slacks and blouse. There were smudges of dirt across both the pants and shirt, doubtlessly from the amount of travel I endured while unconscious.

The train slowed, preparing for its stop at the facility. My chest tightened as the fate destined for me came closer. Richard stood up, reaching for something behind his back. There was a flash of silver as he brought handcuffs from his back pocket.

I'm sorry I have to do this, Darcy. An order is an order. Will you please join me by the doors?

I could see the sorrow in his dark brown eyes as he looked down at the handcuffs in his hands. Rather shakily, I stood to my feet, struggling to find balance in the midst of my nausea and the train coming to a stop. Making my way to Richard, I allowed him to place my hands in the cuffs behind my back. His hands were gentle as he guided my arms where they needed to go.

Whispering into my ear, Richard leaned forward from behind me.

Whatever happens today, I want to let you know that I'm proud of you.

My eyes became misty just as the doors to the train opened, revealing the facility's underground station. Guards stood immediately outside the doors, waiting for my arrival. To my surprise, Margot was nowhere in sight.

Richard greeted the guards and guided me onto the platform outside of the train. The guards nodded to him in respect before grabbing the cuffs behind my back and pushing me to the same doors that Margot had led me through weeks before.

Over my shoulder, I looked back at Richard, his sad eyes following me as the guards roughly pushed me to the secured doors. One of the guards raised a card to the scanner at the door. With a quick glance, I saw Margot's name printed across it. Though she hadn't been there for my arrival, her card had been forfeited to the guards for access to the facility.

The doors opened to the same eerie hallway that led to the elevators. Gripping my arm tightly, the guards pushed me toward the elevators and scanned Margot's card once again. Shifting as it moved from its position, the elevator took us up to the main level.

As the bell rang notifying us of our arrival, memories of the facility broke free of the dam I had built to hold them back. Memories of Kate, Noah, Margot. Yet, the realization that took my breath away and set my heart to racing was that I was in the same building as Ben.

XIX.

REUNION

Shoving me out of the elevators, the guards kept one hand on my back and one on the handcuffs. Since the tunnels were on the opposite end of the facility as the executive suites, our journey passed by the hallway leading to the gym and classrooms.

We passed several familiar faces of recruits I had trained alongside. They seemed shocked at my return, watching as the guards continued their journey to Margot with me in tow. It must have been close to noon as the perspiring recruits made their way back to their flats. In the small clusters of recruits, I found the faces of Brendan and Sam whose eyes were wide in horror.

Finally, we had reached the hallway to the classrooms, over halfway to the executive suites. As we walked past the opening, Kate and Noah looked up from where they leaned against the wall talking. Kate dropped her books and started toward me. The guards, registering her reaction, pulled me back from her. I pushed against the ground, ceasing all movement of me and the guard holding my cuffs.

The other guard went to block Kate's advancement. She looked over his shoulder toward me, pale in shock.

Darcy! Darcy, are you okay?

Hey, Kate.

Frantically, I pushed against the guard and searched for the right words. It hit me like a wrecking ball: it was time to initiate my plan. The plan that I thought was over as soon as I was deployed. There was no better time. And I didn't know how much more time I had.

It wasn't my plan coming back.

I was hoping Kate realized the meaning behind my off-the-wall statement. To my relief, her eyes lit up when she heard me say the word "plan." Carefully, I nodded to her, maintaining eye contact the entire time. The guards who were both struggling to separate the two of us didn't seem to notice the signal.

Noah came behind Kate and murmured something in her ear. Hesitantly, Kate backed away from the guard and retreated to a safe distance. The guard holding my cuffs had lost his patience with me, jabbing me in my side where my kidney sat. I fell to my knees, searching for breath after his well-placed blow.

You're hurting her. Stop!

Kate's protests only seem to aggravate the guards more who pulled me up to my feet despite the continuing struggle to catch my breath. I looked up to find Kate, but my eyes landed behind her, not on Noah but on the figure standing frozen in place with his face pale and eyes wide.

Ben's shock at my reappearance was obvious. Yet, it was the torment in his eyes that caused the ache in my soul. Flashes of him filled my mind: his green eyes soft with affection, his smile that could brighten up my darkest day, and his warm lips pressed against mine desperately.

Our eyes locked from across the hallway for what felt like an eternity. I didn't know what he was thinking, whether he was still angry with me and had enjoyed my absence or if he had missed me as much as I had missed him. His eyes held too many emotions to explain: fury, desperation, sorrow.

The few weeks I had been gone felt like over a year as I looked down the hall to where he stood watching me. The space between us felt like the entirety of the desert, both emotionally and physically. Then, the guard was pulling me away down the hallway, out of the sight of Kate, Noah, and Ben.

I only hoped Kate could initiate the plan before I ran out of time. The window for our plan working was quite small but no smaller than the chance that I would survive the day. If it was the last thing I did, I was going to take down the Society with me.

It was up to me to buy Kate some time to communicate with the other recruits and for Brendan to trigger the system failure. Dragging my feet, the guard was forced to put more and more pressure on my back to hurry our pace.

After what seemed like twice as long as the first half of the journey across the facility, we had reached Margot's office door. With a knock, her rigid voice commanded us to enter. She stood, hands clasped behind her back, looking out the window toward the horizon.

They sat me down in front of her desk roughly. My hands were smashed behind me, pressing the hard metal of the cuffs into my wrists. Placing the handcuff keys and access card on the opposite side of the desk, they turned and retreated out of the room.

At the sound of the door clicking shut, Margot began to speak while still looking into the distance.

Darcy, you have disappointed me repeatedly. From the start, you have created waves here at the facility. You have created drama amongst the guards, used my nephew, and rebelled against direct orders.

I will accept the responsibility for all those things, but I never used Ben. Blame me for anything else, but not that.

You should have never been involved with him. I have put too much work into him to become an asset to this Society. I will not let some blonde orphan off the street mess with his head and ruin all of my work.

Her hard exterior was beginning to break down as I continued to resist her reprimanding. I persisted in pushing her, hoping it would buy us more time.

He came to me.

She walked over to her desk briskly, putting her hands on the top and leaning toward me. Her eyes burned with fury, sparkling in the heat of the moment.

You would learn to keep that mouth of yours shut if you knew what was good for you. Evidently, you have this issue since you are back here after a failed mission.

I did what was best for me. I'm not a killer like you.

Margot sat down in her chair, smirking to herself. She looked over at me with years of wisdom and experiences flashing across her face.

You have no idea what I've done. Perhaps you wouldn't be so rebellious of my authority if you knew.

Enlighten me.

Her face revealed that she was not the type of person to turn down a challenge. She sat upright in her chair and placed her elbows on the desk, hands folded neatly in front of her.

Well, as you know, there are some events that happen in the world naturally. However, many of the events that have shaped humankind are the events that we created. I, myself, have ordered countless events including terrorist attacks on consulates, outbreaks of severe illnesses, and mass school shootings.

Why? I thought the Society was created to help people.

That is what my sister and her husband created it for. They were always too soft, too compassionate. The world does not deserve that. In fact, I believe they were hurting the world in the long run by prolonging problems. Illnesses, famine, war, they all happen for a reason: to control Earth's population.

She paused and looked down at her hands, then back to me. Her eyes were sharp and determined.

The reason for the world's detriment is overpopulation and lack of proper government. We can fix that. The Society is the answer.

You think you're helping the world by killing innocent people? You really are crazy.

I have seen countless people helped by the events we create. For instance, Ben...

Her sentence ended abruptly as she seemed to realize what she was about to reveal.

Never mind, that is none of your concern.

No, what about Ben? What did you do to him?

She bowed her head, focusing on the top of the desk. Moments passed before she continued the conversation.

Since I'm going to kill you today, I guess it doesn't matter if you know or not.

Know what?

My chest tightened as she drew in a breath to begin her confession. I feared what she had done to Ben.

In the midst of it all, I couldn't help but marvel at the animalistic protection that mates held for one another. Ben with his bloodying of Connor and me with my desire to claw Margot's eyes out.

Realizing the pause our conversation had taken, I redirected my attention back to Margot who had swiveled her desk chair so she could look out at the barren desert landscape.

My sister and her husband created this Society, thinking their benevolent mission could positively impact the world. However, I always had my doubts. They recruited me to manage this facility including the training regimen, recruits, and guards. But I did not have a voice. Refusing to succumb to my theory on what could help the world, they merely continued with their trips to help the needy and kept me locked away here.

Margot was no longer present in the room but thousands of miles away in her mind. She sat glaring out the window.

They were always well-liked by everyone. I was always in the background. No one could see they were only helping the detriment of society. And one day, I had enough. Overriding their need for approval, I ordered one of our members to stir up a rogue militia group in South Sudan where they were rebuilding a village.

You killed them? You killed your own sister? Ben's parents?

I did what had to be done. They were only making things worse and refused to take my advice.

That's because you're an insane murderer and they were nice enough to love you past it!

Love? You're just as stupid as they were. Love is weakness, merely a cause of failure.

So why did you take in Ben after you killed his parents? Why not just kill him too?

She sneered, throwing her head back in amusement.

I see that I'm going to have to spell this out for you.

Yes, please do.

Her sharp looked showed her impatience with my sarcasm.

Ben had potential. As soon as I took charge of how he was raised, I taught him to be strong. Taught him that love is weakness and that if you let people get close, it only gives them easy access to a knife in your back. He was a perfect soldier until you came around, you little twit.

He was just a boy at the time, not a soldier! He had just lost his parents! He needed comfort, not to be taught to push everyone away. It's not love that makes you protect him, it's the work that you've put in to making him a machine.

The smirk on her face was anything but regretful, more victorious. My stomach churned as I thought of Ben as a small boy, his parents just murdered by his aunt. He didn't know. He'd never know.

Now, let me call the guards in so we can perform your execution elsewhere. I wouldn't want to get blood on the carpet, I'm quite fond of it.

She pressed a button on her phone to send request to the guards' beepers outside the door. After a moment, when no one entered, Margot pressed the button again impatiently.

Guards!

When no one answered, she rolled her eyes in exasperation. Getting up from her chair, she started to walk out from behind her desk when she stopped short at the sound of the door opening. She looked horrified as her eyes looked toward the door, nearly stumbling backwards into her chair.

Clueless of the reason for her reaction, I turned my head to look toward the door. There stood Ben.

Benjamin, dear, I'm in the middle of something. I'll have to ask you to return later.

He stood staring at Margot, speechless and stoic. No emotion could be read on his face, only dark green eyes.

Ben?

The sound of my voice broke his stare at Margot as his eyes flickered to me. His eyes lost their guard. They were shattered like glass, his whole world turned upside down. Then, I realized: he knew.

After seeing me in the hallway, he must have followed us to her office and listened outside the door. My heart was heavy, wanting only to run across the room to embrace him, to hold all of his broken pieces together. Hug the young boy who had lost his parents much too early, who had been raised by the person who murdered his parents.

Margot seemed to realize something was off, again pressing the intercom button to request a guard. Ben turned his attention back to her.

They won't come. They're knocked out in the hallway.

Margot stood her ground, not flinching in the slightest. I could see she was afraid to assume what all he had heard. She waited for him to speak again.

Is it true?

What are you talking about, Benjamin? Honestly, your behavior is quite troublesome.

You killed my parents.

I don't know what you're talking about. Darcy has filled your head with lies.

No. Drop the act, Margot. I heard the entire conversation. You admitted it. You killed them.

She stood trapped, caught in her lies and guilt. Worse yet, she didn't seem regretful or defeated at all, only cautious.

You always taught me not to trust anyone but all along, you were the one I should've trusted the least! All along, you were the one who killed them.

Now, Ben, what I did was necessary for the Society, for the world.

How can you make an excuse for killing your own sister?
My parents helped people. You think that your murder, war, and
diseases are helping the world? It's only making it worse!

It really is a shame that after all the work I put into you,
you still turn out just like your parents. I was afraid of that.

Margot reached for the phone, pressing a single button.
She brought it to her ear, still watching the both of us. Ben stood
shocked by her blatant disregard of the murder she committed
while I still sat, hands cuffed behind my back.

Please come to my office. My guards have been
incapacitated. Come now.

Ben walked closer to the desk, nearly within arm's reach of
where I sat. His attention was still on Margot as she stood behind
her desk, unflinchingly returning his stare. She reached into her
desk drawer, pulling out a gun.

His body tensing even more than before, Ben went on
defense as soon as he saw the firearm. His hands went up cautiously,
letting her know she didn't have reason to shoot.

Margot, you don't have to shoot anyone. No one else needs
to get hurt.

She seemed unaffected by anything he said, pointing the gun
straight at me. Her eyes were fierce as she glared over the desk.

I change my mind. This carpet needs updating anyway. It's
time to get rid of you. You've caused all of this. Everything was
running smoothly before you showed up.

Ben slowly moved closer to me, attempting to come in between me and Margot. His hands were still raised near his chest in defense.

Ben, move out of the way or I'll kill you first.

Put the gun down, Margot. This is not the answer.

Her hand had become slightly shaky as she stood with the gun pointed straight at Ben. Peeking around him, I could see that she felt hesitation in killing him. Though she attempted to seem emotionless, I could see that she cared for the boy she had raised.

Suddenly, there was the sound of footsteps from the hallway, hard and fast. I turned to look at Margot's help and nearly fell out of my chair. There stood Connor, with a gun in his hand pointed straight at Ben.

XX.

SHUTDOWN

Connor, thank you for joining us.

What little patience Ben had left went out the window when he heard Connor's name. His body shrugged slightly in disappointment at his arrival. Turning sideways between the two but still protecting me from Margot, Ben looked between Connor and Margot.

Seriously, Margot? Why Connor?

Connor is a fine soldier. Loyal. He has kept me updated with your involvement with Darcy.

It took everything in my power not to laugh at her approval of the imbecile. Thinking that a laugh or insult might push one of the gunmen to their limit, I chose to keep my mouth shut. Ben could already use help without me angering anyone more.

As I caught on to her last statement, my stomach churned at the idea of Connor reporting everything he saw between Ben and me. Stealing a glance toward Connor, I found the same cocky grin on his face as so many times before. Only this time, the gun pointed at Ben made it impossible to ignore.

Connor, please escort Darcy out of here and take care of the mess you make when killing her.

Before I could stand up, Connor advanced toward me and grabbed my arm roughly. The other hand still pointed the gun straight at Ben.

No, no!

I fought hard against him as he dragged me out of the room, scraping the floor with my feet in resistance. His grasp on my arm only tightened as we got closer to the door.

Margot, stop. Please.

Ben's voice was shaky as he turned from watching Connor drag me away to look at his aunt. He glanced desperately between Margot and me, looking helpless.

Hold on, Connor.

Connor looked furious as she halted his progress toward the door. Margot seemed to be thinking over her options, her distraught nephew obviously causing doubt in her plans.

Are you kidding me? I'm sick of him getting away with everything!

Quiet, Connor.

No. I'm sick of it.

Margot looked incensed as Connor interrupted her train of thought. Suddenly, the sound of a gunshot deafened the right side of my face. Blood poured down the front of Margot's blouse. Her face was shocked as she crumpled to the floor.

Ben ran to his aunt's side, feeling her neck for a pulse. She lay still on the ground, unblinking. Horrified, he stood up and looked to where Connor held the gun straight at him.

I'm so sick of you getting your way. Your aunt can't help you now, can she?

You stupid piece of sh—

Now, now, Ben. We wouldn't want anything to happen to your little tramp, now would we?

Connor moved the gun to my temple, pressing it into the already tender bruise. Ben froze in place, ceasing any advancement toward us.

Leave her out of it. Your problem is with me.

You should have never been head of the guards. It should have been me. The only reason you got the job was because of your aunt. Well, I'm in charge now.

Then fight me. Once and for all. Let's settle it. Man to man. No guns. Just us.

Connor took some of the pressure off my temple as he contemplated Ben's challenge. I knew deep down that his cockiness would get the best of him, as it always had.

Fine. Then, you get to watch me blast your girlfriend's brains out of the side of her skull.

Deal.

Ben knew exactly what he was doing as he managed to persuade Connor to release me for the fight. All too quickly, Connor pushed me toward the desk and caused me to fall hard on my knees.

Ben looked down at me right before the lights shut off. The red emergency flashing lights began to blink, illuminating the room in eerie color. Then, suddenly there was noise behind me as Connor threw his gun down and sprang into action. Ben blocked his advance and began striking toward Connor.

While the two were engaged, I scrambled toward the desk in search of the handcuff keys. They still sat where the guards had placed them. Carefully, I turned my back to the desk and searched for the keys with my cuffed hands.

The cool metal grazed my fingertips before I was able to grab them from the desk. Meticulously, I felt around for the keyhole on the cuffs, scraping metal against metal until the key slid into place. As the cuff on my right hand loosened, I wiggled it free and brought my hands forward to unlock the other hand in front of me.

Dropping them to the ground, I snatched the access card from the desk and searched for Ben in the midst of the red flashing lights. The two of them took turns striking toward one another and then blocking the other's advances.

Hearing the cuffs drop to the ground, Ben took a quick glance over to me. Suddenly, he turned his attention back to his opponent and furiously struck Connor right in the nose. As always, Connor bent down in agony with yet another injury to his nose.

Ben ran over to me in the quick moment he had before Connor recuperated. His warm hands gently squeezed my arms as he looked me over for injuries.

Are you alright?

Yeah, I think so.

Then, suddenly he was kissing me, desperately and passionately. Had it not been for our current situation, I could have just melted in his arms. It was over as quickly as it began.

You have to go, Darcy. Get out of here.

Come with me.

No, I have to stay.

You don't understand. We rigged the building to blow. Kate, Brendan, Sam, and I, we had a plan all along.

He took a moment to absorb the information before recalculating his plan.

Well, we can't do anything with Connor coming after us with a gun. I'll meet you down in the tunnels. But you need to go now. Get everyone else.

I'm not leaving you, Ben. I'm not losing you again.

I'm right behind you. But they need you now. Take the access card, it's the only way.

He pushed me toward the door as Connor stood up, blood dripping down his chin. In the red flashing lights, he nearly looked insane.

Darcy, I love you. Go.

Connor began to advance once again, harder and faster than before. Ben took a hard blow to the ribs as he blocked me from the punches. With one last glance back, I ran down the executive hallway toward the elevator.

Desperately, I ran toward the tunnels. Kate and the others had done a wonderful job of spreading the news as I failed to see anyone on my way across the facility. The elevator that took me down to the tunnels must have been hooked up to the backup generator since it was still operational.

As soon as the elevator doors opened, I saw dozens of recruits packed into the long hallway leading to the station. The secured door was the only obstacle between them and their freedom.

Familiar faces filled the crowd of people as I pushed through to the security checkpoint. I scanned the card and the doors creaked open to the station. The subway car sat on the rail, waiting to be taken out of the facility.

Several of the recruits disabled the few guards that advanced on the crowd, attempting to stop the rebellion. Then, my eyes caught a figure close to the entrance of the train. Richard. I put my hand in the air to ward off any recruits from approaching him.

I walked toward him, hands in the air as a sign of peace. His eyes looked concerned as he scanned over the group of people waiting to board the train.

Hey, Richard.

Darcy....

So, you know when you said that the Society couldn't be taken down? Well, it's happening. And you're the only way that we're going to survive. We need to get out of here before the building blows.

He looked down at the ground as he assessed the situation. His brow was furrowed as he glanced between me and the crowd of recruits and staff members.

I knew it'd be you.

Grinning from ear to ear, he clapped me on the back and motioned for the recruits to board the train. I nodded to them, letting them know it was okay. One by one, they filled the several subway cars that lined the tunnel.

Kate came out from the crowd and grabbed my arm. She threw her arms around my neck.

Oh, Darcy, I missed you so much! I was so worried about you!

I pulled away as Brendan, Sam, and Noah approached us. They nodded in greeting to me before Kate began to spill every detail.

Right after I saw you in the hallway, I went and got Brendan and Noah got Sam. Brendan triggered the system to shut down while Sam and I placed the timed explosives under the support beams. The entire time, Noah was spreading the news to the recruits and to the staff members. Whether they agreed with us rebelling against the Society or not, they didn't want to be here when the bombs went off.

And the message to the members in the field?

Brendan sent it out right before the system went down. But there's no way of knowing how any of them will react.

How did you get the elevator to bring you all down here? I thought you needed an executive pass.

The elevators were connected to the main grid, so Brendan was able to disable their security requirements. But, like he said before, he couldn't hack into the tunnels.

I looked around at my co-conspirators proudly. Somehow, we had done it.

Have you seen Ben? We couldn't find him anywhere.

Immediately, the sense of pride for our plan vanished as I realized that Ben wasn't there yet.

He's up in the President's office, fighting Connor.

Wait, what?

I'll fill you in later. I've got to go get him.

Pushing my way past Kate, she desperately grasped at my arms.

No, Darcy. There's no time.

She looked at her watch and then toward the last of the recruits filing into the train.

We only have two minutes before the first bomb goes off. Then, it will be a chain reaction until it reaches the tunnels. There's no time to go across the facility. He's probably on his way now.

But what if he's not?

Kate went silent as she thought about the possibility. Noah stepped toward us, putting his hand on Kate's back.

Darcy, he is very skilled. I have no doubt that he knocked Connor out moments after you left. He is most likely on his way. We need to get in the train.

But...

We will wait until the very last moment before leaving. He'll be here.

Brendan and Sam walked toward the subway car first. Noah and Kate each took one of my arms as they gently led me to the double doors. I couldn't help but look back at the secured doors that had been jammed open by some of the recruits.

No matter how hard I prayed, Ben still hadn't walked through them. Seconds turned into minutes until it was too late. Looking absolutely destroyed, Kate put her hand on my back.

Darcy, we have to go or we'll all die. He's not going to make it.

I couldn't lose him again. The thought of living life without him gave me no reason to leave. I would die here alongside him. As I went to sprint out of the train, Noah intercepted me and wrapped his arms around me in restraint.

The subway doors closed, and I felt the car begin to move. I fought against him, but it was like beating down a wall.

No! No! I have to go to him! No!

At the top of my lungs, I screamed desperately. Tears streamed down my eyes as I continued to beat against Noah. Loud blasts reverberated off the walls of the train and I knew it was too late. He was gone.

I dropped to my knees in agony, sobbing uncontrollably. Kate sat beside me, wrapping her arms around my shoulders as I wept. Noah stood over us, wiping away the stray tears that rolled down his cheeks.

Ben, my Ben! No, no, no...

No matter how much I begged or sobbed, the train continued its path away from the facility. The loud blasts continued to follow us as scheduled. My sobbing only grew deeper and more desperate the more I thought about Ben and his sacrifice. The damage to the facility was of no comparison to the condition of my heart, crumbled and burnt, never again to be repaired.

XXI.

AFTERMATH

I couldn't help but think that the agony in losing a loved one is the finality of death, the utter permanence of it. At the age of nineteen, I had endured many deaths, grieved for too many people. Ben's pushed me over the edge.

Flashes of that train ride still flicker through my head. The pain in my throat as I screamed at the top of my lungs, the desperation to save him, to undo the finality of his absence.

If I had known he wasn't going to make it to the train, I would have stayed or dragged him with me. Had I known it would have been the last time that I ever saw or touched him, I would have never let go.

Yet, no matter how much I knew that this type of thinking wouldn't change anything, I couldn't help but repeat the same thoughts in my head over and over again. If... Had I...

Kate had stayed by my side the entire train ride with Noah hovering nearby. Others stayed away, unquestionably giving me space as my entire world crumbled around me. Near the end of the train ride, I had lost every ounce of energy in my body and had grown silent, collapsed on the floor.

Richard emerged out of the crowd of recruits; his brow furrowed. Sitting right beside me on the floor, he stretched his legs out straight and leaned his back against the door of the train. I lay on my side, curled up in the painful agony burning my insides.

His hand patted my back as he gazed off into another world. My breathing was still slightly uneven as I lay next to him on the floor, silent. Then, after a few moments, Richard cleared his throat and spoke low enough for only me to hear him. Kate had gotten up to give us privacy whenever he had approached, speaking softly to Noah nearby.

You didn't tell me you loved him.

Memories of our plane ride together filled my thoughts. I had only told Richard that I knew Ben, not the extent of our relationship. Words had long escaped my abilities as I lay there utterly defeated. He seemed to realize that I wasn't going to reply and continued talking.

Years ago, I attended the memorial service for Ben's parents. I remember seeing the small boy, lankier than I had seen him months before. His hair was long and shaggy, hanging into his eyes. He stood by his aunt next to the caskets, head hung low.

Richard paused, his eyes in the past. He looked down at his hands in his lap.

I couldn't imagine the loss he felt that day. Knowing the last thing he wanted to hear was that I was sorry for his loss, I walked up to him and shook his hand. He looked up at me with bloodshot eyes and I remember telling him, "Your parents left this world helping people. That's what makes a hero. You never forget that, son."

I pictured young Ben heartbroken next to the caskets of both parents, next to their murderer.

In my book, Darcy, he's done that exact same thing. He went down a hero today. His actions saved the lives of every single person on this train and so many more. I'm not telling you all of this to interfere with your grieving, I just wanted to let you know that he will be remembered by many.

He paused to let me absorb his statement. Then, I heard him stand up from the ground, grunting slightly as he stretched his back. Before he walked to another part of the train, he looked down one last time.

Take all the time you need, Darcy. But when it's time, don't forget you have a life to live, a life to spend helping others.

In the time following our escape, the recruits scattered across the country. Some retained the trade they had learned during training. Brendan remained in IT, landing a job in Boston, Massachusetts. In addition, Hannah realized her passion for government and moved to Washington D.C.

Still yet, others decided to make an entirely new life for themselves. Sam decided architecture was not what he wanted to do for a career and decided to backpack across the world looking for his dreams. The last postcard I had received from him illustrated the cliffs of Ireland.

Little did we know at the time, Brendan had not only depleted the funds for the Society, but rerouted it into a bank account which he later split between all of the recruits. The money helped every person with their travel expenses, housing costs, and basic needs for the first few months while they readjusted back to civilian life.

I traveled back to my hometown in Oregon, searching for any feeling of home. Noah and Kate followed me there, hoping to help support me in my time of mourning. Though I tried to persuade them I would be fine, Kate insisted she wanted to see where I grew up.

For the next couple of weeks in Oregon, I attempted to find any kind of normalcy. After finding out about a secret society that influenced the world, there was no place paranoia did not follow me.

On a sunny afternoon, Kate attempted to brighten my day.

Darcy, why don't you go to the store? I need a few things for dinner tonight and it will be good for you to get out... and get out of sweats.

Oh, thanks, Kate.

I'm sorry but laying around, crying in your pajamas all day isn't helping you. Get some fresh air.

With a small amount of grumbling, I threw my hair in a bun and got dressed in jeans and a t-shirt. Walking down the street to a small grocery store, I found myself observing my surroundings often. I eyed several people on the street and looked behind my back.

Finally, I stepped into the grocery store and found the few items Kate needed for dinner. By the time I made it to the cash register, I was sure the entire store was in on the conspiracy to kill me.

The cashier looked up at me, noticing my nervousness. His red, curly hair and freckled face hovered above his name tag reading "Larry."

You from around these parts?

Yes.

Oh, I've never seen you around here before. You just move closer to the store?

His friendly small talk only persuaded me more that he was trying to squeeze information out of me. I froze in place, looking down at the items on the counter. He seemed to realize I was uncomfortable and took my money. Grabbing the bag, I quickly walked out of the door and made my way back home speedily.

Kate was shocked to see me sprint back through the door, dropping the bag of items on the counter and retreating to my room. She seemed to sense I had been pushed too far by something and left me alone.

It was later that night after I had skipped dinner when Kate burst into my room. Instead of the compassionate and soft-spoken Kate who comforted her grieving friend, I found the same blunt and sassy girl who I had met in the flat that first day at the facility.

Darcy, that's enough. I'm sorry but this isn't good for you. You lay around all day, crying and refusing to eat. You looked panicked from a short run to the grocery store. This isn't healthy.

What do you want me to do, Kate? Forget about the fact that I destroyed a Society that may still have loyal followers everywhere?

They would have no way of finding you. We destroyed their communication and network holding necessary information to operate. They have nothing.

You know, I never did see their board members. Where are they? You don't think they could figure out how to rebuild?

My voice had become rapid and desperate. I breathed heavily as panic began to flood into my veins. She put up her hands to stop me from continuing.

Darcy, calm down. It's over. We destroyed everything. They can't find you.

I wish Ben were here. He would know for sure. We could hide where they would never find us.

Ben wouldn't have wanted this. He would've wanted you to keep living, not paranoid that everyone is out to kill you.

She wiggled her hand in her back pocket before pulling out a slip of paper. Handing it to me, I unfolded it and found a phone number.

That's Richard's number. He told me to give it to you whenever you're ready to help the world.

Kate watched me for a moment as I looked down at the paper, unsure whether I was ready to help others. I heard the door click shut as she left the room, leaving me drowning in questions with no answers.

Two weeks later, Richard took my luggage out of my hands to load into the car. Kate and Noah stood waiting for their goodbyes as Richard closed the trunk. I looked at both of them, smiling.

Now, Darcy, you promised you would be back in time for the wedding. You are the maid of honor, so you have no choice.

Noah smiled down at Kate as she spit out her words at an incredible rate in excitement.

Yes, I promise. Richard and I are going to South Sudan for a month and will be back here right in time for the rehearsal dinner.

Are you sure you want to go to South Sudan, Darcy? Isn't that where Ben's parents…

That's exactly why we chose to help rebuild villages there. I intend to continue the work they started.

Noah stepped down from the curb with his arms spread wide for one of his famous bear hugs. He squeezed me tight and looked down at me, smiling.

Ben would have loved that. Good luck, bud.

Thanks, Noah. Take care of her, will you?

I nodded my head in the direction of his fiancée who already had stray tears running down her cheeks. Before I could reach her, she jumped off the curb and wrapped her arms around my neck.

Be careful, okay? Just because you were trained by Noah to kick people's butts, doesn't mean you should go around picking fights, alright?

Man, why am I even going now?

Both of us laughed, hugging one last time before I left.

Love you, Darc.

Love you, Kate.

Richard shook Noah's hand and hugged Kate before getting in the driver's seat. I waved, looking back over my shoulder at my two favorite people in the world.

Love had a way of finding light in the darkest moments of life. In the wreckage of the Society's collapse, the death of a loved one, and restarting a life, love not only survived but thrived. I only hoped my love for Ben would help me to influence the people of South Sudan.

XXII.

INKLING

You're back! Oh, I've missed you!

Kate ran toward me in a floral jumper. She was absolutely glowing as she welcomed the guests to her rehearsal dinner. It was a small event, with a couple of local friends she had made and some of the recruits including Sam, Brendan, and Hannah. I waved to their smiling faces from across the room as Kate hugged me tight.

In my absence, Noah had reached out to Kate's parents and persuaded them to come to the wedding. Having been outcast by her extremely traditional parents, it meant the world to her to have her family back and supportive of her marriage. They stood in a new conversation with Richard in the opposite corner of the room.

So, how was South Sudan? Kick anyone's butt?

No, Kate. I was there rebuilding a village, not on a mission to take out their rogue militia groups.

I know, I know. Just thought it would make for an exciting toast.

She smiled at me before pulling me into conversations with others. Many of them asked about my trip across seas. I was glad to share the inspiring experience I had and listen as Richard told it from his point of view.

Over the course of the trip, Richard and I had become very close. In many ways, I looked to him as a father figure. He helped me grieve Ben in a healthy way, protected me, and helped me past the obsessive paranoia that had consumed me since the shutdown.

The small group of us sat around a beautifully decorated table. White tablecloths and winding ivy accompanied gold rimmed china plates and crystal glasses. The sophisticated yet natural design of the entire room was the perfect definition of Kate.

Noah and Kate sat near the head of the table, totally engrossed in one another and their guests. The glow of the candles on the table illuminated the faces of everyone around their dinner. Well into the meal, I tapped a knife against my glass and stood from my chair. All eyes were on me with the anticipation of a toast.

I just wanted to say a few words about my two favorite people in the world. Never have I seen two individuals so absolutely in love with one another. Through all of the obstacles life has thrown you, there has not been a moment of doubt, a moment of separation.

The faces of the fellow recruits looked toward me knowingly, doubtlessly remembering our days at the facility. For me, the hard part came after leaving. As my thoughts began to gravitate toward uncontrollable tears, I redirected the closing of my toast.

I wish you many more happy years together. To Kate and Noah.

The entire room was filled with the clinking of glasses. I looked over toward the happy couple as Noah lifted his glass in the direction of Sam's glass. My eyes were immediately drawn to the same scar many of us shared, the scar where our tracking devices were once planted.

Yet, for some reason, my eyes traveled to the inside of his bicep. To my surprise, I found nothing there. I sat back in my chair and continued my dinner, deep in thought.

Ben had a tattoo on the inside of his bicep, a random assortment of letters and numbers. Of all the nights we spent in the same bed, I had fallen asleep many of them while reading those characters over and over again. They were forever engrained into my memory.

I had never asked Ben what the letters and numbers meant, assuming each guard had an identification number. But Noah didn't have one. His other arm went to prop up on the back of Kate's chair, revealing the bareness of his other bicep. My brow furrowed in confusion.

Kate looked over at me, noticing my concerned expression. Her gaze was confused then soft as she seemed to have come to a realization. She must have thought the sappy speech had reminded me of Ben. Quickly, I smiled her way and continued eating my food, unable to keep a prolonged conversation with anyone as thousands of thoughts ran rampant around my head.

Later in the evening, the guests were scattering to their vehicles after saying their goodbyes. After finishing her conversation with her parents, Kate walked up to me smiling.

It was a great rehearsal dinner, Kate. The food was delicious, and it was good to see the old classmates again.

Yeah, I almost didn't think Hannah or Brendan would be able to make it across the country, but they had some vacation days they were able to use.

Well, that's good.

Alright, Darcy. What's going on? I saw your face after the toast. You want to talk about it?

I shook my head in disagreement, shrugging off any serious concern she may have had.

No, it was nothing. I'm just tired. You know, jet lag. I'm going to go and crash on my bed.

Okay, well I will try to be quiet when I come home tonight.

No need. I'll be passed out.

We both laughed before I started to walk toward Richard's car. He stood leaning against the driver's side looking up at the stars. When I approached, he looked down with heavy eyes.

I don't know about you, but I'm beat.

Yeah, me too. Thanks for the ride home. I really need a car.

It's no problem. Your luggage is still in my trunk anyway and it's on the way to my hotel.

We both shut the doors of the car behind us before he started the engine. The headlights illuminated the vehicle's bumper in front of us.

How long are you planning on staying in Oregon?

My plane leaves in the morning.

Oh, and are you planning on settling anywhere or continuing to travel around the world?

I haven't made my mind up yet. I'm thinking about going home to Texas, got some family there. Might buy a ranch there, get a cow or dog or something.

A cow?

He chuckled and threw up a hand from the steering wheel jokingly. Making a right turn, Rich pulled up to the apartment that Noah, Kate, and I shared. Of course, he insisted on getting my luggage out of the trunk and carrying it up to the door.

Outside of the entrance door, I threw my arms around his neck. He squeezed me tight and kissed the side of my head.

Take care, sweetheart. You ever need me, you call. You know the number. I'll be here in a second.

Thanks, Rich, for everything.

It was my pleasure. Maybe we can make it an annual trip. There's always someone needing help in the world.

Sounds good. But who will take care of your cow when you're gone?

He laughed as he walked back to his car. As he pulled away from the apartment, he waved at me. He didn't drive away until I had opened the apartment door. I knew he still had issues with paranoia like me. It was something we had bonded over while in South Sudan, something we helped each other through.

Though I had told Kate I would be collapsing as soon as I was home, my mind was much too active for sleep. In my room, I found the cheap laptop I had bought to help me research South Sudan before my trip.

I opened the browser and started typing frantically. If the tattoo on Ben's arm was not an ID number every guard was assigned, then what was it?

I was not expecting to find the meaning of those letters and numbers so quickly. However, as the first search appeared, pictures of hills and countless evergreen trees littered the screen.

The numbers and letters were not any kind of identification at all, but coordinates. Yet, the coordinates did not have decimal places that made it an exact location. Instead, they merely pertained to a small region in the foothills of Idaho.

The rolling hills and lush forests were beautiful, providing elevated views and breathtaking sunsets. Besides the picturesque beauty of the landscape, my exhausted mind couldn't figure out why Ben would have coordinates tattooed on his arm. It had been strategically placed where no one would be able to see it without his sleeve rolled up or his arm extended.

I collapsed on the bed, still trying to find the reason. However, sleep consumed me immediately and cut my thoughts short.

My dreams were the same as every night: filled with images of Ben, memories of our time together. Although my agony returned as soon as I woke up, the dreams provided a temporary relief from the pain.

Ben rolled over on his side, his smile creating the tiniest crinkles around his eyes. He bent his head down to where I lay, kissing my shoulder and then my neck, gradually reaching my lips. His soft, warm lips lingered over mine.

I closed my eyes and let him surround me, his strong arms wrapped around my body. My nose was filled with his scent, the light scent of his cologne. Rubbing my hands over his bare back, I felt every indentation of his muscles.

He pulled away slowly, opening his eyes to reveal an explosion of color, my favorite shade of green. A grin slowly spread across his mouth.

Tell me about your home growing up.

Well... it was a small two-bedroom home. My mom kind of had simple taste, dainty yet warm. Somehow the kitchen always smelled like freshly baked cookies.

Ben smiled down at me as I described my childhood home. The white cabinets, lace curtains, and the small ways my mom seemed to make it a home and not just a place to live.

I miss that house... and my mom.

His eyes softened as he ran his hand along my cheek, following his touch with his eyes.

I know.

So, what about your house?

We didn't really have a house. We moved around a lot. Apartments, hotels, and villages overseas.

But what about that cabin? The secret cabin in the woods?

His eyes glossed over as he was transported back to his parent's cabin.

The cabin had three rooms: one for me, one for my parents, and an office for them. There was a large living room with an area rug in the middle of the room. Wood beams ran across the ceilings, a fireplace was centered in the room, and couches were circled around a coffee table that had been roughly made of logs.

Ben smiled as he remembered his family in their cabin, still looking off into the distance. His room was silent as he paused.

I remember my dad would be working on blueprints and itineraries for trips in the office. He was never angry if I interrupted him, only put me in his lap and taught me about his projects. My mom would be in the kitchen making hot cocoa for us.

What was your favorite part about the cabin?

He thought for a moment, deliberating how to choose his favorite spot. It was obvious that the answer dawned upon him as the corners of his mouth curled upward.

The cabin was on top of a hill, surrounded by trees so that it was secluded. But if you went to the right spot, the trees opened up over the hill to the most beautiful view. During sunsets, the entire horizon was covered in beautiful, rich colors. It would give the landscape a golden hue, the trees, the grass, and even the mountains in the distance.

Sounds amazing.

It was. Anytime that my parents would look for me, they always found me there.

I wish we could go there now.

Yeah, me too.

I shot upright off my bed, my heart beating rapidly in my chest. My breathing was heavy and uneven as I looked around my dark room. Then it hit me. The coordinates, the tattoo, the dream, they all led me back to the same place: Ben's cabin.

XXIII.

CABIN IN THE WOODS

The next morning, I woke up to the alarm on my phone. After waking from the dream, I tossed and turned all night as sleep came in small quantities. Each time I closed my eyes, images of a golden landscape would fill my dreams.

Suddenly, Kate burst into my room still in her pajamas. Her dark hair was pulled into a braid over her shoulder and her cotton shorts bore the design of Snoopy.

I'm getting married today!

She jumped on my bed, jostling me up and down with her movement. Finally, she plopped down beside me. In her hand was a small white box with flowers engraved over its surface.

I wanted to go ahead and give you the jewelry to match your dress before everything got too crazy. I decided on pearls. I thought they would go nicely with the wine-colored bridesmaid dress.

I'm so glad you went with a fall wedding. I love the colors.

Well, I didn't want you to look like a pumpkin, so I avoided orange at all costs.

Thank you for that.

We giggled together before she handed me the box. I opened it, catching sight of the beautiful necklace and matching earrings. Speechless, I couldn't help but think of the pearl necklace that Ben had given me some months back.

I know it's not the necklace he gave you, but I wanted you to feel like he was here today.

The words caught in my throat as tears began to fill my eyes. I nodded in appreciation as she sat waiting for my response.

Thank you.

You're welcome, babe. Sometimes, I wish I had kept that necklace. Giving it back only hurt both of you.

I cleared my throat of the tears and furrowed my brow in confusion.

What are you talking about?

Well, I saw how much you wanted to keep it that day you told me to give it back to Ben. And now, you don't have it to remember him.

Yeah, but you said it hurt the both of us. What do you mean?

Her face became solemn as she remembered her encounter with Ben months ago.

Well, I didn't see him in the hallway when I went to classes that afternoon when you were deployed. It wasn't until the next morning that I saw him. He was stoic as ever, coming in right before class and starting immediately. I kept the necklace in my pocket for the entire class.

Kate pushed some of the loose hair from around her face, continuing with her story.

After he dismissed everyone, I walked up to him. He looked only slightly surprised that I approached him. I took the necklace out of my pocket and told him you wanted me to give it back, that you didn't feel right taking it.

She looked down at her hands in her lap, nervously picking at her fingernails. Her pause felt like an eternity as I waited to hear more about Ben.

I'd never seen him look so broken. He was always so guarded except around you. Around you, he seemed happy. He just took it and nodded in thanks. When I walked away, he was still standing there looking at the necklace in his hand.

My chest was heavy as I felt the pain I had caused Ben by returning his mother's necklace. Images of his broken expression burned into my brain. I pat Kate on the leg, making her look up from her nails.

Hey, it's your wedding day. Only happy tears today. Let's start getting you ready!

The day went by in a blur of hair, makeup, and dresses. Noah had stayed the night with one of his friends, so the apartment was covered in everything female.

Kate looked gorgeous in her dress, lace running down most of her arms and the top of her back uncovered. Her hair was pulled up with soft tendrils hanging here and there.

My hair was down, its golden strands cascading down the wine-red floor-length dress. Luckily, Kate's short train was easy to manage as both of us climbed into the car on our way to the wedding.

She had chosen the perfect wedding venue, a small chapel in the woods. The crowd of people gathering there was small, sitting on the wooden benches facing the front of the chapel. I could see Noah standing near the front of the crowd next to the officiant.

Kate looked nervous as I went to open my door first. I reached to hug her, careful not to mess up either of our hair or makeup.

You look so beautiful, Kate.

Thanks, Darc.

You nervous?

Yeah, I don't know how to explain it. I know I want to be with him the rest of my life but it's a big decision, you know? It's a day we'll remember for the rest of our lives.

Well, you better not keep him waiting then. I'm sure he can't wait to see you.

She smiled, looking out the window toward where he stood before the crowd. When she nodded to let me know she was ready, I opened my car door and circled around the back to open hers.

Kate was right. It was a day I would remember for the rest of my life. I would forever remember the sweet words of their vows, the way Noah's face lit up as Kate walked down the aisle with her father, the height of the trees towering above us. It was a day none of us could have imagined only a few months before.

Kate and Noah spent most of the following week vacationing near the coast for their honeymoon. During the time they were gone, I was packing my few belongings in suitcases and boxes. With some of the money I had left, I bought an old, yet dependable SUV.

When Kate and Noah arrived back home, I greeted them with enthusiasm and questions about their trip. They both seemed happier than ever before, looking refreshed from the week of vacation.

Letting them tell their many stories, I sat and listened patiently to their shared experience. Then, after Kate caught her breath and Noah leaned back on the couch, I chose to break the news to them.

I'm moving out.

Wait, what?!?

Kate did not seem too pleased by my sudden confession. Cool and collective Noah even sat up from his spot on the couch.

You guys are married now and need your privacy...

No, Darcy...

Let me finish. And I need to be on my own. Since the Society, I've had you guys and Richard. But I've realized that I need to support myself, learn how to live alone without anyone's help.

Darcy, you can't move out. Where will you go?

I'm thinking about taking a trip before finding a place to settle. Don't worry, I'll visit a ton. I just think it's time.

Noah cleared his throat and rubbed Kate's back, who at that moment, looked like she was going to explode.

Well, Darcy, we accept your choice and appreciate your respect of our privacy. Just be careful and don't be a stranger. You'll always be welcome to stay here.

Kate shook her head but couldn't hold back the tears that threatened to spill down her cheeks.

Oh, Kate, don't do this. I'll be fine.

I'm just going to miss you, Darc.

I'm going to miss you too, Kate.

When do you leave?

In the morning. I've already got everything packed.

She nodded and wiped a stray tear from her cheek. We spent the night as we had always done since our days in the flat, sitting in the kitchen and talking over Kate's delicious dinner.

Though so much had changed in the past month, I couldn't help but realize the many things that hadn't changed: friendship, love, off-the-wall conversations, Kate's enthusiasm. Though it wasn't goodbye forever, I would still miss them every single day of my life.

The road seemed endless as I continued my journey east from Oregon. My phone was programmed to tell me the directions based on the coordinates I had plugged in for the destination.

It was around a five- or six-hour drive until I reached the circumference of Ben's coordinates. Since they weren't exact, I would have to search in the area for any heavy wood cover on a hill. As if that narrowed down much of my search.

Finally, I reached the coordinates tattooed on Ben's arm. I searched for thickly wooded areas and parked on the side of the road. Pulling my backpack from the passenger seat, I stepped out of the car and headed toward the woods.

My hiking boots plodded against the surface of the ground as I continued to travel uphill. The knife holster on my hip rubbed against the top of my thigh. Occasionally, I would grab my water bottle from my bag, stopping for a drink and to track my location.

It was nearly an hour into my walk when I found a small path leading up the hill. Following its course, I found that it opened into a clearing. The shade of the trees and the fall breeze provided temporary relief as small amounts of sweat gathered on my temples from the hour of climbing uphill.

Looking around the clearing, I found a cabin near the back of the small field. It was a generously sized building made of large logs with a porch running around its entire circumference. As I made my way to the back of the clearing, I noticed it looked uninhabited.

Stepping onto the front porch, I knocked on the door and waited for anyone who might have lived there. There was no way to know whether I had found the right cabin.

After no one answered the door, I walked around the porch and looked for any sign of residents. Finding an entrance in the back, I took one last glance around the property before twisting the doorknob.

To my surprise, the door opened into a large living room. My heart skipped a beat as my eyes caught familiar objects: the coffee table made of logs, the fireplace, and the large area rug. Ben's words echoed in my head as I walked around the interior of the cabin.

Walking through the living room and kitchen, I found pictures of Ben and his parents. I studied their features. Ben was built like his dad but had the coloring of his mother. They all looked so happy together in their pictures of various holiday celebrations or with villagers from another country.

I continued to the bedrooms. One of the rooms was obviously intended for a young boy, a small bed in the center with various toy boxes and a small desk placed around the room.

Inside the next bedroom was a formidable king-sized bed with large wooden posts on each of its corners. Pictures of Ben's parents were hung all around the room. The bedside table held a single frame with a picture of the two on their wedding day.

Making my way down the hallway past the bathrooms and coat closets, I found the last room to be an office. A window with its blinds closed took up a large part of the exterior wall. I made my way to the window and opened the blinds, allowing natural light to illuminate the room.

A long bench sat under the window, a perfect spot to sit and enjoy the view of nature or read a good book. In the corner, a drafting desk looked out at the view of trees and wildlife.

I turned from the window to make my way to the desk when my leg hit the bench. The bench sounded hollow, echoing the strike of my foot. Grabbing the top of the bench, I pulled upward and discovered a storage space. Inside were several blueprints, a lockbox, and a couple of guns.

I grabbed one of the blueprints, making my way over to the drafting desk so that I could spread out the paper. The blueprint was similar to the one back in the facility that Sam had shown to me, the same one we used to plan the Society's downfall.

It was obvious this copy was an early edition, with some of the rooms not accurately depicted. Yet, one thing caught my eye: a tunnel. But it was wasn't the same tunnel we had escaped through, but one right under the executive suites.

I stopped my mind from wandering as I found other discrepancies with the blueprint. Several classrooms were missing and there weren't enough floors for the recruit dorms. It must have been an early edition before the final plans were put into place. Rolling it back up, I placed it back exactly where I had found it and returned the lid to its original place.

My eye caught sight of the picture frame beside the desk, a picture of a young Ben overlooking a beautiful sunset. He sat on a tree stump near the edge of a hill, looking at the horizon. It was the same golden sunset he had described to me before, more beautiful than I could have imagined.

I looked out the window of the office and saw a path leading into the woods. Other than the path that I came from, it was the only other opening out of the clearing. It must have been to Ben's infamous hideaway.

Longing to feel close to him, I made my way back outside and followed the trail. The sound of birds singing filled the air as the crisp fall breeze shook the colorful leaves of the trees surrounding me. My hiking boots crunched the dead leaves and twigs beneath my feet.

A short walk from the cabin, the path opened to the same small viewing area in the picture. The afternoon sun illuminated the color of the hundreds of trees below. Rich fall colors filled the landscape, producing a golden paradise.

My eyes followed the familiar sights from the picture, the curve of the hills and the shape of the horizon. Turning around, I searched for the tree stump on which to sit.

For a moment, I thought I was looking at the picture again. My sight was filled with the same image, Ben sitting on the stump overlooking the view. But this time, Ben looked much different. This Ben was not a child, it was Ben as I knew him.

I blinked hard to rid myself of the illusion but found the same sight every time. Clearly, I had finally gone insane. Not only were my dreams haunted by images of him, but now every waking hour.

Yet, it wasn't a Ben I had seen before. He wore a flannel shirt, worn jeans, and hiking boots. His hair was slightly longer than I had ever seen it. The tone of his skin was tanned as if he had been in the sun and he seemed free. There was no longer any guard, no walls to keep anyone out.

It couldn't have been a dream. Though he was my Ben, he was too different to be a memory. In the midst of my observations and confusion, he seemed to notice my presence and stood up quickly, mirroring my shock.

There was a moment as our eyes met, as we both tried to persuade ourselves of the truth, of its possibility. Then, it wasn't the gold, orange, and red of the trees that filled my vision but green. My favorite shade.

Made in USA - Kendallville, IN
1050851_9781702419604
02.24.2020 0752